After all these years, how can Hanna face her long-ago date to her disastrous last cotillion...?

"As you well know," Pastor Jacobs said, "we have been searching for a youth minister for our junior high and high school students. Someone has answered our call, and he is with us tonight. This particular man comes to us with high recommendations from the Dallas area. He isn't married, and he says that God hasn't put that special someone in his life yet. At this time let's give a warm Houston welcome to Abundant Grace's new youth minister, Mark Alexander."

Hanna felt the blood rush from her face, and her eyes grew wide. *It can't possibly be,* she told herself. *It must be a coincidence of names.* Memories of her high school days and the all-consuming crush she had on Mark Alexander made her spirit plummet. Slowly, she lifted her head and fixed her gaze on the man mounting the steps that led to Pastor Jacobs. The way he carried himself looked too familiar.

As soon as he turned and faced the crowd, her fears were confirmed.

DIANN MILLS lives in Houston, Texas, with her husband Dean. They have four adult sons. She wrote from the time she could hold a pencil, but not seriously until God made it clear that she should write for Him. After three years of serious writing, her first book, *Rehoboth,* won favorite Heartsong Presents historical for 1998. Other publishing credits include magazine articles and short stories, devotionals, poetry, and internal writing for her church. She is an active church choir member, leads a ladies' Bible study, and is a church librarian.

Books by DiAnn Mills

HEARTSONG PRESENTS
HP291—Rehoboth
HP322—Country Charm

Don't miss out on any of our super romances. Write to us at the following address for information on our newest releases and club information.

Heartsong Presents Readers' Service
PO Box 719
Uhrichsville, OH 44683

The Last Cotillion

DiAnn Mills

Heartsong Presents

I'd like to thank the following writers for their support, encouragement, and helpful critiques: Andrea Boeshaar, Gloria Brandt, and Sally Laity.

A note from the author:
I love to hear from my readers! You may correspond with me by writing: **DiAnn Mills**
Author Relations
PO Box 719
Uhrichsville, OH 44683

ISBN 1-57748-785-0

THE LAST COTILLION

Cover design by Robyn Martins.

PRINTED IN THE U.S.A.

prologue

"I heard Mark say that Hanna's dad paid him to escort her tonight."

"I'm not surprised. What guy would come with her anyway?"

"Well, I think it's really sad. It's her last cotillion. And her father had to pay someone to take her. I feel sorry for her."

"Not me! I'd sew my mouth shut before I'd get that fat. Did you see her dress? It looks like the sheers over my grandmother's bay window."

Hanna heard both girls giggle. She slipped out of the ladies' room before the girls realized she'd heard every word they'd said. Her breath came in short spurts and hot blood rose in her face. *Dad paid Mark Alexander to escort me,* she silently repeated. A lump rose in her throat, and she fought the flood of tears. *I wanted tonight to be perfect, something I would remember forever. Tonight was supposed to be special, and now, Daddy has made me the laughingstock of the whole senior class.*

Humiliated and hurt beyond measure, Hanna wanted to leave immediately, but she had to hear the truth. Did she dare wait and ask her father. . . ? No, she desperately needed to know now. She would ask Mark. Maybe the girls had heard a lie. Her gaze tore through the crowd, searching for the special group of kids where he could be found.

And there he stood, his broad shoulders leaning into the girl beside him. The girl, a curvy cheerleader, broke into laughter. He grinned his famous dimpled smile, revealing his perfectly straight white teeth, and shoved his hands into his tux pockets. He teetered back and forth on rented, shiny black dress shoes, obviously enjoying every flirtatious moment.

Hanna cringed. Just the mere sight of Mark's dashing good looks always sent her senses into a tailspin, ever since her freshman year. Now, she envisioned the gold sparkle in his deep brown eyes, the sheen in his black hair. He nodded in her direction, and his cordial acknowledgement filled her with contempt.

The whoosh of Hanna's legs brushing together announced her arrival to the group. Instantly their chatter stopped, and she felt their eyes upon her, mocking and memorizing her every gesture.

"Mark, can I talk to you a minute?" she asked crisply.

"Right now? I'm sort of busy hanging out with my friends." He gave his captivating grin to the girl beside him.

Hanna heard one boy snicker, and she saw other smirking faces. They had been discussing her, she felt certain.

"This is important, and I need to talk to you now," Hanna said firmly. Her voice sounded strange in her ears. She bit her lip, holding back the angry, caustic words that spilled from her lips all too often. This time, she told herself, she would not lose control. Mark appeared irritated, but she didn't care. "Excuse me," he said to his friends. "I'll be right back." He followed Hanna to a secluded corner away from the noise of the others.

She looked into Mark's brown eyes and tried desperately to control her whirling emotions. "Look, I've just heard that my father paid you to escort me tonight. Is this true?" She almost spit the words at him, her eyes burning with hurt and rage.

Long, anxious moments followed while she studied every inch of his chiseled face. Hanna understood his silence; she waited for his charm to dictate the proper reply. He shifted his feet and his eyes darted about like a trapped animal.

Hanna turned away. "You don't have to answer," she said, barely above a whisper. "I already know the truth." And then, unable to help herself, she turned back and screamed at him, her anguish and fury spilling out of her in a torrent.

one

Hanna Stewart nervously tapped the carpet with the toe of her high-heeled shoe while she waited for her turn to sing. As the organ and keyboard played a duet, she prayed that the words and the music would glorify God. But no matter how many times she sang, solos always turned her stomach upside down, even when she sang in church. Even though she had performed for years, she was always nervous beforehand. Now, brushing back her abundant hair from her face, Hanna licked her lips and willed the uneasy sensations in her stomach to stop.

Perhaps singing should *make me nervous,* she reflected. *It keeps me leaning on God rather than myself.* When the music minister nodded for Hanna to take her place, she took a deep breath and prayed one last time.

Hanna had chosen the song "Friend of a Wounded Heart." From the first time she heard it in the church choir, she had claimed the song as her own. The words were her testimony, and when she sang it, passion rang from each note. The song had brought her through the long months of dealing with her eating disorder and the destructive behavior that accompanied it. The words had filled her soul with a longing for God and a desire to place Him first in her life, and Hanna had at last learned to eat and exercise properly—and allow God to heal her heart.

Once the song began, she relaxed and concentrated on the opportunity to praise God with her voice. When she finished, the congregation applauded, and Pastor Jacobs, a balding, older gentleman, thanked her. She humbly seated herself in a pew and opened her Bible in preparation for the sermon. *Thank You, Lord. Thank You for everything You've done for me.*

"We have someone special to introduce to all of you tonight," Pastor Jacobs announced. His tall, muscular frame and booming voice always commanded everyone's attention. While listening to his every word, Hanna retrieved her journal and pen to take notes on the sermon.

"As you well know," Pastor Jacobs continued, "we have been searching for a youth minister for our junior high and high school students. Someone has answered our call, and he is with us tonight. He will be available after the service to meet with you, especially the youth and their parents. This particular man comes to us with high recommendations from the Dallas area. He isn't married, and he says that God hasn't put that special someone in his life yet. At this time let's give a warm Houston welcome to Abundant Grace's new youth minister, Mark Alexander."

Hanna felt the blood rush from her face, and her eyes grew wide. *It can't possibly be,* she told herself. It must be a coincidence of names. Memories of her high school days and the all-consuming crush she had on Mark Alexander made her spirit plummet. Slowly, she lifted her head and fixed her gaze on the man mounting the steps that led to Pastor Jacobs. The way he carried himself looked too familiar. As soon as he turned and faced the crowd, her fears were confirmed.

Mark Alexander smiled, and a flood of humiliation and regrets washed over her, stinging the old wounds she thought were healed. For a brief moment she walked the halls of high school again, reliving her pain. Gathering up all of her courage, Hanna blinked and forced herself to look at Mark. The overhead lights picked up the shine in his jet-black hair, still so thick and shiny, just as she remembered. His shoulders seemed broader, and the face of a man replaced her recollection of a teenage boy. He waved to the crowd, and Hanna's heart skipped a beat. She felt like a sixteen-year-old again.

I thought I'd gotten over that silly schoolgirl crush, she scolded herself. *It's been nine years, and he still affects me the same way.* She took a deep breath. *Dear God, I know I've asked You to forgive me for all the things I said and did back then. I was so bitter and self-centered. But this, Lord. . .I can't bear seeing Mark again.*

From somewhere deep within, Hanna thought she heard the voices of all those kids in high school making fun of "Hippo Hanna," the class joke. But she pushed away her thoughts from the past; best to forgive and forget. She recollected all too well how full of sarcasm, selfishness, and bitterness she had been back then. She should apologize to Mark.

How can I? she asked herself frantically. Facing him would be the hardest thing she had ever done. What if he could see she once cared for him? She had hid her feelings well in high school, but that was the old Hanna—without the Lord.

A sudden question rose in her mind so strongly that she turned her attention to Mark and studied him while he related his background to the congregation. *What happened to change him?*

She knew his family had struggled with an alcoholic father and a mother who worked herself much too hard in order to support Mark and his brothers and sisters. He had done well in sports, and there had been rumors of a football scholarship. Something must have turned him around, for the Mark Hanna remembered was not a Christian.

As Mark's greeting came to an end, Hanna shifted her attention back to Pastor Jacobs and scolded herself soundly for permitting her thoughts to wander. For the rest of the service she focused her attention on the message.

❧

The welcoming line for those who wished to greet Pastor Mark Alexander grew shorter and shorter. Hanna had taken a place at the very end, hoping the extra time would provide her with insight into what she should say. First she prayed, and then she attempted to piece together the right words for an apology. She remembered all too well the way she had screamed at him at the cotillion ball. Trembling, she feared bursting into tears in front of him. She inhaled deeply and massaged her slender arms. Why did she feel so cold? The air conditioning inside the church must have been turned low. Why else would she be freezing? The line moved much too fast. Couldn't these people linger a while longer?

Hanna braced herself. Why hadn't she gone home? But as youth music director, she had a responsibility to welcome Mark. *Oh, God, help me get through this.* If only she had known ahead of time the name of the new youth minister, then perhaps she could have prepared herself.

All too soon, Hanna reached to shake Mark's hand but then thought better of it. Too late; before she could pull back her hand, he grasped her damp, cold fingers with his.

"I thoroughly enjoyed your song," he said warmly with the dimpled grin she well remembered. His olive skin glistened with health and vitality, and his deep brown eyes still held the same mysterious gaze that seemed to read her heart. "It was beautiful."

"Thank you." She paused, nervously nibbling an inside corner of her lip while she mustered strength to continue. "How are you, Mark?" Her words sounded shaky and distant.

His questioning glance flew to hers.

"Remember me?" she asked. "High school days?"

He shook his head, clearly confused. "I'm sorry, but I don't."

She smiled. She didn't know whether to be hurt or relieved. "It's Hanna, Hanna Stewart."

Surprise and astonishment shone on every inch of his handsome face. He stood speechless. "You've changed," he finally managed, wetting his lips.

"And so have you." She laughed nervously.

"We will have to get together and talk. I often wondered what happened to you."

"Old times are one of the reasons why I'm at the end of this line." She took a glimpse around to make certain the crowd had filtered away from them. "Mark, I am sorry for all the cruel things I said to you and your friends when we were in high school. Can you forgive me?" She spoke much more confidently than she felt.

His eyebrows rose. "Forgive you? How can you ask such a thing?"

Hanna froze. Could it be she had just opened an old wound of his?

"I wronged you, not the other way around," he assured her. "I am the one who needs to be forgiven."

"I don't look at the circumstances in quite the same way. I was selfish, cruel, nasty, and I didn't know the Lord," she explained. "I am ashamed of the way I acted."

Mark relaxed slightly. "I am the one who is ashamed. I never thought I'd see you again—and I needed to apologize for my horrible attitude."

"Now we both can." Hanna suddenly realized they were still holding hands. He must have sensed the same thing, for he instantly released hers.

Embarrassed, Hanna glanced in the direction of a gathering crowd of students and parents. Neither of them seemed to know what to say next.

Pastor Jacobs joined them and placed his hand on Mark's shoulder. "I see you have met our youth music director." The senior pastor tipped his head in Hanna's direction.

"So you are the one Pastor Jacobs has raved about." Mark gave another blue-ribbon smile. "I've been told you are the best youth music director this church has ever seen."

"Oh, no," Hanna denied. "The kids are great; I just guide them along."

Mark turned his attention to the pastor. "Hanna and I went to high school together."

"Is this the first time you've seen each other since then?" Pastor Jacobs asked.

"Yes, and it looks like both of our lives have headed in the right direction." He gave Hanna his full attention. "Perhaps we could sit down soon and talk about everything, from high school days to the church's youth. If you don't mind, you could really help me get to know the students."

Hanna's heart pounded furiously inside her chest. *He wants to get together?* But she didn't want to help Mark Alexander; she didn't want anything to remind her of those miserable high school days. A stab of guilt struck her, though. Where would she be if everyone still judged her by her past behavior? She would have to try to look at Mark Alexander as though he had never hurt her, as though he were someone she had just met.

Taking a deep breath, she replied, "Of course, I'd be happy to help."

Pastor Jacobs chuckled. "Well, Hanna does a splendid job with our students. They have never sounded better, and she has terrific skills at pulling the kids together."

Pastor Jacobs' voice echoed in her ears. All she wanted to do was get away from Mark. "I'd better let you visit with the students and their parents," she managed. "They're waiting to talk to you."

"Right," Mark said. "Can I call you as soon as I get settled into my office?"

"Sure, the church directory has my number."

Hanna watched Mark disappear into the crowd of parents and students. Never, absolutely never, had she dreamed of seeing him again. Well, perhaps he had been in her dreams once or twice, but nothing had prepared her for this confrontation. What had made him commit himself to the ministry? When did it happen? He looked so happy, and somehow that bothered her; a part of her wanted him punished for stealing her heart away. *This is wrong,* she told herself, but he had hurt her so badly. The memories all came back again, carrying with them the same old heartache.

She realized then the impact of what Pastor Jacobs and Mark

had been saying: She and Mark would be working together with the youth! The thought set off an ear-piercing alarm inside her head, and her face grew warm with a slow blush. How could she team up with him after all of these years? She didn't want to have a thing to do with him. Memories of sharing chemistry lab rippled across her mind, and she bit her lip, remembering how she had used sarcastic words to hide her heart from him. Could they both put the past behind them and go forward with only the students' well-being in mind? Hanna had never found herself both so curious and so apprehensive at the same time.

In the church's foyer Hanna saw her friend, Marie Trace, and her husband talking with another couple. Marie worked as the high school receptionist where Hanna taught music, and the difference in their ages hadn't stopped them from becoming close friends. The tall, large-boned woman stepped into Hanna's pathway now.

"Are you all right?" Marie studied her carefully with warm gray eyes. "You look pale."

"I feel like I just saw a ghost," Hanna whispered, glancing around to see if anyone else could hear their conversation. She smoothed her long, flowered skirt and tugged on her vest, although neither article of clothing needed adjusting.

"A ghost? What do you mean?"

Hanna took a deep breath. "The new youth minister. . . well, we went to high school together."

"Is knowing you in high school so bad, or is there something more to it?"

"To tell you the truth, I had a terrible crush on him."

"Oh, no," Marie breathed. "How uncomfortable for you."

"Now it appears we will be working together with the youth," Hanna replied miserably.

Her silver-headed friend gave her a look of motherly concern. "And how are you going to handle it?"

"I'm not sure. The shock hasn't worn off yet. I might leave town." Hanna made an attempt to laugh.

"Did he recognize you? I mean, does he know who you are?"

Hanna tried to laugh. "Yes, but he didn't until I told him. He wants us to get together to talk."

"Sounds like you're off to a good start."

"I suppose so, but it doesn't stop the fluttering in my stomach. Marie, I don't want a thing to do with him. The very thought makes me ill. I feel as though I—"

"Unless," Marie interrupted, with a knowing smile, "you're still carrying a torch for him."

"Of course not," Hanna quickly replied. "I'm a grown woman. Maybe I'm just embarrassed because he knew the old Hanna."

"But you knew the old Mark, too," came the gentle reminder.

Hanna sighed and shifted her shoulder bag. "If only the new youth minister could have been anyone but Mark Alexander."

Marie looked sympathetic. "I'm sorry, dear, but it will work out, you'll see. Are you going home?"

"Yes, I need to prepare for school tomorrow. The spring concert is in two days, and some of the music sounds rusty. I guess I'll see you in the morning." Hanna flashed her friend a quick smile and headed for her car.

❧

Sleep eluded Hanna that night. She needed her rest to teach the next day, but the day's events continued to torture her mind. At first she toyed with the idea of calling her parents: *Guess what? Do you remember Mark Alexander? He's our new youth minister.* But she couldn't bring herself to make the call. Her parents would be thrilled to hear Mark had committed his life to the ministry, and Hanna desperately wanted to be genuinely happy for him. At least she wanted to believe she felt goodwill towards him. The truth was, she didn't know how she felt about him.

At one time, he had been the white knight in every one of

her dreams. She had fantasized that he chose her above all the other girls in school. Her body was a hundred pounds over-weight, but her heart loved him with all the emotions a teenage girl could embrace. When they were juniors, they had shared chemistry lab, and Hanna thought she'd found heaven. Of course, he never knew how she felt; she was careful to hide her feelings, but still she placed him on a pedestal. She had cherished their friendship until the night of the last cotillion. Even now, the memories from that night were too painful to dwell upon. She had forgiven her father; after all, her family did not know Jesus then. But had she ever forgiven Mark? Maybe she still felt afraid of the past, hovering over her like a black cloud.

Hanna knew one thing for certain. Her relationship with the Lord took top priority. When she surrendered her life to Him, her very existence changed. She had vowed that nothing would ever stand in the way of God's will for her life again.

Hanna punched her pillow as though it were to blame for her sleeplessness. *Am I so low as to want Mark's life to be a failure?* she asked herself. *Am I some sort of sadist who wants him to be miserable? Surely not! But do I really want Mark to be a part of my church?*

She sighed. *Not my church; God's church. Could Marie possibly be right? Am I carrying an old schoolgirl crush?*

"God forgive me," Hanna cried out loud. "But I never wanted to see him again. How can I continue my music ministry with the students?"

She didn't want to quit her job as youth music director. Those kids were a part of her life. Could she abandon them because she felt uncomfortable around Mark Alexander? Certainly not!

Mark has changed. A still quiet voice spoke to her heart. *He knows Me.*

But You have no idea how he hurt me, her heart cried back. *I can't work with him and ignore my feelings. . .especially when I don't even know what they are.*

two

Mark placed the last box of books on his desk and seized the opportunity to sit down and explore his richly paneled office. He hadn't expected the cherry desk or matching bookcases—or, for that matter, his very own secretary. In the past, he'd used whatever a church could afford and appreciated it, but this looked so good that it scared him.

Lord, I don't know what I've done to deserve such finery, but thanks. He opened his planner and glanced at all the things he wanted to accomplish today. No way could he manage half of it. A couple of items jumped out at him, one of which had kept him up long past midnight.

Hanna Stewart, daughter of Hal and Anna Stewart—her father, one of the wealthiest men in Houston, and her mother, an ex-model. Both were pillars of society, yet he couldn't remember if they were Christians. Mark sighed deeply, recalling his last encounter with Hal Stewart and the money. . . Oh well, he couldn't change a thing, and praise God he was finally able to apologize to Hanna last night after all these years. Just the thought of her sent a strange chill up his spine. She was. . .gorgeous! Odd, he didn't remember her eyes, so violet and tear-shaped, or her full lips. And that long, thick, caramel-colored curly hair. When did she make such a complete transformation?

Most important, he had seen a sparkle of real peace in her eyes, and when she smiled, her face mirrored a sweet, sweet Spirit. *Nearly knocked me for a loop.* He shook his head. *Hmm. . .Hanna. Her name means grace.* He thought back to high school when they shared chemistry lab. If it hadn't been for her, he'd have flunked for sure.

He didn't understand the peculiar stirring in him, unless it was old memories. . . Yes, it must be the past and the countless times he wished he had not taken the money from her dad.

He wanted to call Hanna, but what would he say? He needed to set up his office, put together the youth gathering on Wednesday, schedule the parents' meeting, and a thousand other things. But soon, very soon, he'd call Hanna Stewart.

ა

The next few days Hanna was busy with year-end work at Pine Forest High School. Grades had to be turned in, plus a mound of filing loomed on her desk. The spring concert had been a success, but a bittersweet pang surfaced as she considered the upcoming graduation. She would never again see some of the kids she'd nurtured for the past four years.

She was so proud of her students, especially Preston Taylor. Hanna smiled, remembering her first day teaching music and how the young man, then a freshman, had stirred up more trouble than she could recount. During the month of September he had disrupted every class, shoe polished the word *fatso* across the windshield of her car, and if that wasn't enough, he had proceeded to let the air out of her tires. Hanna had wanted him removed from her class, but the vice principal encouraged her to give him another chance. Soon afterward Hanna gave her life to Christ, and Preston became a challenge instead of a thorn. She supported his musical endeavors and offered him piano lessons. Through her support of his talent, his single mom and two younger sisters came to Christ. Now Preston had obtained enough grants and scholarship money to finance four years of college.

"Are you ready for school to end?" Marie asked Hanna one afternoon after the students were dismissed. The two sat across from each other at a table in the teachers' lounge.

Hanna rested her chin in her hands. "Yes and no," she admitted. "The break sounds wonderful, but I feel like I'm pushing my baby birds out of the nest."

"You've had other classes graduate," Marie commented.

"I know, but these kids have been with me since day one of my teaching," Hanna replied pensively. "And, well. . .this summer with the church youth may not be my best."

"Why is that? Is there a problem with the youth mission trip?"

"Absolutely." Hanna sighed.

"And?"

"Oh, Marie. I've got to work with Mark on this trip, and the very idea has me scared to death and nearly sick." There, she had said it. Why didn't she feel any better?

"Have you met with him yet?"

Hanna shook her head. "No. It's only been a week since he arrived, but every time the phone rings, I panic."

Marie eyed her curiously. "I think you and I need to have a heart-to-heart talk. Let's go get a cup of coffee."

Hanna reluctantly agreed, and a few minutes later they met at a nearby coffee shop. With their mugs in hand, the two women chose a small table in a secluded corner.

"Okay," Marie began, tucking a silver strand of hair behind her ears. "I'm ready to listen. You haven't been the same since the new youth minister arrived last Sunday. You've been preoccupied and anxious." Marie took a sip of her coffee.

"Wouldn't you feel the same?"

"Probably. Maybe you need to get Mark out of the cobwebs and deal with him. Sweetie, you know anything you tell me is strictly confidential."

Hanna took a deep breath and smiled at Marie's words. How many times had she encouraged her students to talk about their problems? And now Marie was using the same techniques on her. She took a breath. "Remember I told you about how miserable I was in high school?"

Marie nodded.

"There's more to it." Hanna hesitated and sipped her decaf coffee. "Marie, I know you're from the West Coast, but do you know what a cotillion is?"

Marie shrugged her shoulders. "Isn't it some type of a formal ball where debutantes are introduced to society?"

"Pretty much. Cotillions were big where I grew up. My parents had me involved in cotillions all during high school. They meant well, but I really looked out of place carrying a hundred extra pounds on the dance floor. Anyway, in the spring of a girl's senior year, at the last cotillion, she is presented by her father. It's very elegant, very special, and very formal. The girls are all in white, and the invited guests are instructed to wear prearranged colors in their formal gowns and styles of tuxes. To make a long story short, Dad wanted me to have the best time of my life. So, he arranged for—or rather paid—Mark Alexander to escort me."

Marie's gray eyes softened. "No wonder you're a case of jitters. It sounds like a girl's worst nightmare."

"Believe me, I felt hurt and angry for a long time. Well, there's more," she continued. "Not only was my weight the source of jokes and ridicule, but I also had a crush on Mark all through high school. Naturally no one knew, but that didn't change my feelings. As a junior, I worked in the school office as a volunteer. Once, when no one was around, I looked up his class schedule and then I made sure our paths crossed. Of course, he had no idea what I'd done. I changed my lunch period to match his and I took longer routes to my classes. He played a very important part in my life, and I spent a good bit of my time daydreaming about him—or rather the both of us. I used to have this fantasy that one day I would wake up skinny and beautiful. Mark would notice, and we would have a happily-ever-after romance."

"How sad for you." Marie's voice sounded sympathetic. "You really had it bad."

Hanna nodded. "Now the sound of his name brings back all of those painful memories. I feel so embarrassed, as though he knew everything." She sighed, wishing the last week of her life could miraculously evaporate.

"But he doesn't," Marie insisted.

"Well, that doesn't stop me from dreading any encounter with him. I wonder why God has put him back into my life." Hanna shook her head and attempted another sip of coffee, but the hot liquid suddenly made her stomach churn.

Marie took a deep breath. "We all wish we knew why God has certain things occur."

"Do you have any suggestions?"

Marie fingered the paper napkin beside her cup and shook her head. "Not really. . .except I'm certain God wants you to give the whole matter over to Him. Have you searched your heart to make sure you have forgiven Mark?"

Hanna pondered her friend's question. "Yes. And really I have. The unhappy girl from those days is not the one here today."

"Then go on about your business and leave the hard stuff to God."

Hanna laughed softly. "Sounds easy enough."

"Of course it is. You've done some remarkable things with your life since you allowed God to take over. Look at the impact you've made on the students here and at church. And what about the weight-management class you teach? Hanna, you sparkle with love and enthusiasm to everyone you meet."

Hanna met Marie's warm gaze. Her deep insecurities from the past must be surrendered to God. . .but oh, it was so difficult.

"Now," Marie continued, "while you're evaluating yourself, take a good look in the mirror. Those violet, teardrop eyes and the way your face curves into a perfect heart is only the beginning of your beauty. I'd give every hair on my head to have your long, naturally curly hair, and that shape of yours. Trust God with all of this; He won't fail you." She tilted her head to emphasize her words.

Hanna gave her friend a half smile, embarrassed by the

lavish compliments. "The question is, Will I fail God?" she asked dubiously.

Marie leaned across the table. "Young lady, we need to pray about this. Let's finish our coffee and then pray."

≥◐

Hanna entered her apartment in much better spirits. She could handle this situation with Mark. After all, a lot had happened in nine years, and she still wanted to find out how he came to know the Lord. As a mature young woman, she must simply ignore the past and help him with the church youth.

Glancing at the phone, she saw the light flashing twice on the answering machine. Hanna dumped her school papers and purse on the kitchen table and reached to check on the callers.

"Hi, honey. We just called to say hello. Give us a call when you have a chance."

Hanna grinned as she listened to her mother's voice, envisioning her standing perfectly poised, her long blond hair neatly pulled back at the nape of her head, her makeup as perfect as if she had just stepped off a magazine cover. Her mother still busied herself with professional modeling, and Hanna felt proud of her mother. But she hadn't always been. . .

Once, she had resented everything about her mother, including the fact they shared the same color of eyes. But her mother was one of the first to forgive her after Hanna had turned her life over to the Lord.

Putting an end to her musing, she listened for the second message.

"Hi, Hanna. This is Mark Alexander. Would you give me a call? I'll be at the church until five o'clock and then home afterwards. Here are my numbers. . ."

She replayed his words three times before her fingers stopped shaking long enough to jot down the phone numbers. Glancing at the clock, she realized Mark would be home by now. She stared at the phone for a long minute.

I'll put a chicken breast in the oven first, she told herself.

Hanna seasoned the meat, wrapped a potato in foil, and put together a salad, then sat down while her dinner baked. Sipping on bottled water, she contemplated returning Mark's call.

He's probably having dinner now. I don't want to interrupt; I'll wait until later and give him a chance to unwind, she hedged, while her heart drummed furiously. Battling old memories, she couldn't even bring herself to return her parents' call.

After dinner, sorting through student records, and filing music, Hanna checked the time again. *Eight o'clock*. She paused. *This is as good a time as any. The longer I put it off, the worse I'll feel.*

She dialed Mark's home, but in her nervousness she got the wrong number. She tried again.

"Hello?" he answered. Hanna's eyes stayed glued to the sheet of paper where she had written down exactly what she wanted to say.

"Hello, Mark, this is Hanna Stewart. I'm returning your call." She hoped her voice conveyed more confidence than she truly felt.

"Hey, thanks for taking the time for me," he replied easily. "I have a list of questions about the students, and I wanted to take you up on your offer to help."

"Sure, what do you need?" Hanna thought her voice sounded faraway, not really her own.

"Frankly, everything. My list starts with the upcoming mission trip and ends with goals for the summer and fall. I wondered if we could meet over dinner and discuss them?" Mark's voice rang all too familiar to her ears.

"I suppose so," she replied slowly, trepidation already building inside her. "When did you have in mind?"

"Is tomorrow night too soon? I didn't know if you would have already made plans."

Hanna purposely hesitated. There hadn't been anyone significant in her life for a long time, but was she ready for this? Clenching her fists, she replied, "No, tomorrow night is fine."

"Wonderful. Since I don't know my way around this part of Houston, can you recommend a restaurant?"

Does he think I patronize all of the eating establishments in this area? she asked herself, slightly irritated. *I don't overdose on food anymore.*

"It depends on what you want to eat," Hanna replied curtly.

"Truthfully, I asked one of the secretaries at the church office what you might like, and she suggested seafood."

Now what are you doing discussing my eating habits with a secretary?

"Seafood sounds good, and I do have a favorite place. Whom, may I ask, did you talk to?"

Mark hesitated. "I'm embarrassed to admit I can't remember her name. All I know is that she took your weight-loss class and lost thirty pounds."

Hanna smiled to herself in spite of her agitation. It always pleased her to hear someone had successfully learned to manage their weight through a biblically based program. "I think during dinner we might start with memorizing the names of the church staff," she suggested, her voice somewhat kinder than before.

"Great idea. What about seven o'clock? Can you give me directions to your place?"

By the time Hanna hung up from talking with Mark, she had a strange feeling that she had been surrounded by an enemy. Why did she agree to have dinner? She could have easily insisted upon meeting him at his office. Now it looked like they had a date—except this was business really, sort of a work appointment. And they were meeting with a common goal. He needed her help, and the students deserved a youth minister who had their best interests in mind.

Still, what should she wear? How would she act? She should have offered to meet him at the restaurant. Hanna's thoughts ran wildly like a key-wound toy. *How am I going to endure the evening?* she asked herself over and over.

She fretted over Mark's conversation with the church secretary. Hopefully he hadn't mentioned the past. Taking a deep breath to settle her nerves, she decided to make notes about the students in choir and a detailed outline of the mission trip. It might keep her mind off her old, silly, schoolgirl crush.

For a brief moment she wondered if Mark had a steady girlfriend. Pastor Jacobs indicated he was unattached. *Don't even think about it,* she scolded. *You'll just invite heartache.*

By ten o'clock Hanna remembered her mother's message and took a break to phone her parents. "We wanted you to have dinner with us tomorrow night," her father said.

Hanna winced. She adored spending time with her parents, but now she'd have to decline because of her appointment with Mark. "I'm sorry, Dad, I've got other plans."

"Would it be a date?" he asked, and she heard the teasing in his voice.

"Sort of."

"And who is the lucky guy?"

Hanna suddenly had a headache. "The new youth minister. Mark Alexander."

"Um," her father said thoughtfully. "Why does his name sound familiar?"

She closed her eyes.

"Hanna?" her father asked.

"We went to high school together," she finally replied. "Remember the last cotillion?" She regretted bringing up the sensitive subject. The thought of upsetting her tall, teddy-bear dad troubled her.

He moaned. "Mark must have done a big turnaround—but then we all did."

Hanna smiled sadly into the receiver. She had long ago forgiven her father for his part at the dance. "I'm trying to look at the situation with that attitude. After all, we're all new creatures in Christ." She sighed.

"Some things are easier to say than to do, huh?"

"Yes, Daddy."

"Anything I can do?" he asked wistfully.

"Not really. I have to handle this myself, but a prayer would be nice."

"Of course. I'm sorry, honey, for my part in that fiasco. I've often wished I could go back and undo it."

"I know, but it's all in the past. I'm wondering if this is going to be as hard on him as it is on me."

"Considering he's now a minister, I bet so."

"Daddy?"

"Yes."

"I can't help but feel like an insecure, overweight little girl again."

"I loved you then, and I love you now. Besides, you're all grown up and God's little girl, too."

"Thanks, Daddy. I love you." But even as Hanna hung up, the dread over her non-date with Mark refused to go away.

three

Hanna walked through her brick apartment complex toward the jogging trail. Already the spring weather zoomed into the eighties with a promise of a long, hot summer. Her nerves were frazzled from thinking about dinner with Mark, and she desperately needed an early morning run to get rid of some excess energy. This morning she had wakened to the thought of pleading sick, and at the rate her stomach turned cartwheels, it might be true. With school ending and graduation fast approaching, she needed to have a clear mind. Maybe the strenuous physical exercise would calm the fluttering queasiness threatening to ruin her day.

Up ahead stood Mr. Henderson, a retired gentleman who walked the jogging trail every morning. They had established a grand camaraderie, and Hanna looked forward to seeing him each morning. She loved his quick wit and the way his bushy eyebrows twitched when he teased her. He waved, and she noticed a man accompanying him. As she stepped closer, Hanna noted a remarkable resemblance between the two.

"Good morning," Mr. Henderson greeted. "How's my favorite jogger?"

"Great," she replied with a smile.

"Hanna, I'd like for you to meet another Henderson—my nephew, Ryan."

She extended her hand and looked into a pair of pale blue eyes. Wavy blond hair touched his ears, and his finely carved features took her by surprise. "Hi, Ryan. Good to meet you."

"My uncle has talked about you for so long that I had to join him this morning," he said, grasping her hand firmly.

Noting the young man's friendly manner, Hanna smiled

and winked at Mr. Henderson. "And what have you told him about me?"

"Just the truth," the older gentleman replied. "You're beautiful, talented, and run every morning. Ryan jogs, too. So I thought you two could run together."

"I hope you don't mind," Ryan said, flashing an easy smile.

"Of course not," Hanna assured him. "Are you ready?"

The two kept pace together during the three-mile run, talking and asking each other questions. Hanna immediately liked him. She appreciated his gentle voice and the way he seemed to really listen, plus he had a wonderful sense of humor.

She sneaked a sideways glance at him. He wasn't much taller than she, probably five-foot-eight or so, and he had the definite trim features of a runner.

"My uncle tells me you teach high school music and lead the youth music ministry at his church," Ryan said.

"Yes, the combination of the two keeps me quite busy, but I love it. How do you pass your daytime hours?"

"I'm a Christian counselor."

"Oh, that must be interesting."

"Well, it usually chases off the girls. I guess it sounds intimidating."

"Oh, do they think you're going to analyze them?" Hanna laughed.

"I suppose so. Truthfully, I love my work; it's rewarding and gives me an opportunity to share Jesus with my patients."

So Ryan is charming, educated, and a Christian. What more could any woman want? she thought with an inward smile. Except she knew first impressions could be deceiving.

"Do you have a private practice?" Hanna asked.

"Yes, but I basically work with troubled teens out of Spring Hills Hospital."

"Spring Hills has a wonderful reputation. One of the girls from our church spent nearly three months there." She considered mentioning the girl's name but then realized the confidentiality of patient information.

"It's a ministry and a haven for hurting kids," Ryan said. "Our goals include mending every part of a young person— physical, mental, and spiritual." He hesitated. "Excuse me; I'm on my soapbox."

"No, it's quite all right," she insisted. "Your work sounds fascinating, and certainly troubled kids need all the help they can get."

"My feelings exactly." He gave her a nod.

They jogged quietly for the next half mile.

"Do you come here every morning?" Ryan finally asked, breaking the silence between them.

"Every one but Sunday."

"So you would be here tomorrow at the same time?"

Hanna shook her head and grinned. "Truthfully, on Saturdays I'm not here until around eight."

"Mind if I join you then?"

Hanna felt her heart skip a beat. "Of course not."

All the way back to her apartment, Hanna thought about Ryan Henderson. She sang while she showered and dressed for school. He had a charming personality, and he certainly was one of the best-looking men she'd ever met. He appeared to be interested or he wouldn't have asked to meet her tomorrow morning. She felt both flattered and captivated.

Her upbeat mood must have radiated from every inch of her, because Marie immediately took notice when Hanna arrived at work humming.

"What has you so happy this morning?" her friend asked curiously. "It certainly is an improvement over the past week."

"Oh, Marie," Hanna began, then instantly remembered her evening plans. "Oops, I nearly forgot about dinner with Mark tonight."

"When did this happen?"

"Last night. It's not a date; we're just meeting over dinner to discuss the youth group," Hanna said, brushing by the evening's activities.

"Oh really? Is the date why you're floating on clouds this morning?" Marie teased.

"Not really," Hanna took a deep breath. "I met someone very nice this morning."

"It had to be a man," the older woman said wisely.

"Well, yeah." Hanna told Marie all she knew about Ryan Henderson.

"So you have a date tonight with Mark, and another one in the morning with Ryan?"

"No," Hanna laughed. "Neither are real dates, just arranged agenda."

Marie shook her head and pencil at her. "Call it what you want, but in my book you have a date with both men." Then she gave a wry smile. "This could be better than a romance novel."

"You are hopeless." Hanna grinned. "But. . .oh well, let's wait and see."

The day zipped by without one incident—or maybe Hanna had so much on her mind nothing could have interfered with the day. At noon she stopped to reflect on the evening and mentally pictured what she would wear. Common sense told her to dress somewhat conservatively; after all, Mark was a minister. Even so, she always made sure her clothes reflected good taste—not too short and not too tight. Mentally selecting a fairly new spring green vest and matching slacks, she suddenly realized she no longer dreaded the evening.

If it's a disaster, then I'll survive. Besides, I still have an eight o'clock run with Ryan, she told herself. *What am I thinking? Tonight is purely professional and tomorrow is fun. It's silly to compare them.*

After school she played piano until nearly five-thirty. The music helped to soothe her fresh attack of jitters that had begun shortly after school dismissed. A long, leisurely bubble bath and the flow of classical music also calmed her frenzied thoughts.

Usually her makeup went on easily with no forethought, but tonight the brown eye shadow and liner looked plain. She deepened the color and then realized she had forgotten blush and mascara.

I am not nervous, she told herself. *I merely want to look my best.*

Hanna gathered up her notes on the church's students and waited for Mark. Promptly at seven o'clock, the doorbell rang. She nearly jumped off the sofa and her knees shook when she stood. Taking a deep breath with a quick, silent prayer, she answered the door.

Mark wore a navy blazer, khaki pants, and what looked to Hanna like a shaky smile—which surprised her. Hanna couldn't help but remember all the times she had dreamed of him standing at her door.

"Come in," she said, feeling a little foolish, as though he knew about her schoolgirl fantasies.

"You look great," he complimented and dug his hands into his pockets.

"Thanks. Did you have any problem with my directions?" She didn't know what to do with her hands, and she caught herself wringing them like an eighteenth-century spinster.

"No, they were perfect, okay, just fine." He glanced around her living room. "Very nice, classy but homey. Wow, your grand piano is a real beauty."

His comment made her laugh, and she felt the muscles loosen in her shoulders and neck. "Thank you, Mark. I'll admit my piano is my baby." Silence followed, and she wished she had memorized something clever to say. "Would you like a diet Coke or iced tea?"

"No, thanks," he replied. "Um, to tell you the truth, I'm starved. I skipped lunch to have a conference with the parents of one of the students."

"Anything serious?" Hanna frowned. She fretted over the kids as though they were her own.

Mark shook his head. "Can't tell just yet. I haven't met the student, only her mom and dad. I thought you might give me a little insight into the situation later on tonight."

"Sure, shall we go? I'd hate to have you faint from hunger."

He gave her an appreciative grin. "You'd look pretty silly carrying me into the restaurant."

The two walked out into the hot humid evening, typical of Houston but uncomfortable nevertheless.

"Sure is hot for May," he complained.

"Yes, we must be in for a scorcher of a summer," she agreed. *Small talk,* she thought nervously. *I hope Mark has enough questions to keep a conversation going tonight.*

He opened the door of a late-model Ford Taurus—clean and freshly washed. It even smelled of country spice. Hanna hoped her rehearsed demeanor hid her fears from the past.

Mark fumbled with his keys. *He's more nervous than I am,* she realized with amazement.

"Can you give me. . .directions to the restaurant?" he asked a bit hesitantly.

Suddenly Hanna found the situation a bit amusing. What had happened to Mr. Cool, Mark Alexander?

"Of course. Do you know the way to the mall?"

"Um, okay, I can get there."

"The restaurant is on the opposite side of the street just past the railroad tracks."

He nodded and stuck his keys into the ignition. "Sounds simple enough."

She wondered about his apprehension. "Mark, may I ask you something personal?"

"Sure, go for it," he replied rather quickly.

Hanna wet her lips. "Why are you so nervous?"

Mark cringed. "Is it that noticeable?"

"Afraid so."

He took a deep breath. "All I can think about is the cotillion thing we went to in high school and. . ."

"How awful it was," Hanna finished.

"Exactly."

"Didn't we apologize the other evening?"

"Yes, but forgiving is one thing and forgetting is another," Mark pointed out. "It doesn't help when—oh well, forget it."

She laughed slightly. At least they could vent their fears. "Now you have sparked my curiosity. Please finish what you've started."

"The truth?" He took a hasty glance at her, and she saw a worried line crease his forehead.

"Yes, Mark, the truth, no matter what it is."

"Well, I started to say it doesn't help when you are so gorgeous."

She thought he sounded irritated. "Would you rather I looked and acted like I did nine years ago?" She felt her jaw tense.

"No," he instantly replied. "Hanna, I meant it as a compliment. It came out all wrong. I meant the apology would have been easier if you were the way I remember."

"Oh, I understand," she quipped. "If I was still overweight, then an apology would have felt more kind and merciful, is that it?"

"No!" Mark fairly shouted.

"You missed your turn," Hanna said, attempting some sort of composure.

"Great," he muttered.

Neither of them said a word while he turned around.

"Guess I need to explain myself," he said quietly after a few moments.

"It wouldn't hurt," she replied lightly.

"In high school, you were, well, different—and I'm not just referring to your outward appearance. All these years, I kept telling myself if I ever saw you again, I would ask forgiveness for being such a jerk. Then this totally knockout of a lady introduces herself as Hanna Stewart, and I wonder what happened to change her, I mean you. All day I've been nervous and anxious about tonight. I feel as insecure as a teenager."

Hanna allowed Mark's words to settle before she replied. The last thing she wanted to do was argue. It looked like her response would set the pace for the rest of the evening—and for their work relationship as well.

"All right, I'll be truthful, too," she said with a sigh. "I've been nervous thinking about tonight, what we'd say and if we could be friends. I am very interested in what brought you to the Lord, just like you are about me. We have a big job ahead of us with the youth at Abundant Grace, and we really need to get along and understand each other."

He pulled his car into the restaurant parking lot and flipped off the engine. "Let me make a suggestion. We could tell our stories since graduation from high school, and maybe then we can call a truce and be friends."

"Deal," Hanna said with a genuine smile. "I'll let you go first."

Once inside the restaurant, while Hanna and Mark waited for a table, he began his story.

"The summer following high school graduation, my father died in a terrible accident. He'd been drinking and wrapped his car around a tree. Mom had a pretty hard time of it, but his life insurance money helped pay off our home and a number of other financial worries. Then in the latter part of August, I left for Texas Tech on a football scholarship. I really thought I was something special. Girls, parties, and football were my life. Of course, I studied, too, but my heart lived for the party scene." He shook his head. Hanna recalled his high school reputation for drinking and wild parties. She listened intently while he continued.

"The summer between my sophomore and junior year, a friend invited me to a Campus Crusade for Christ meeting. I didn't want to go, but my friend threw in a steak dinner before-hand. So I went—and it seemed to me like the speaker knew me inside and out. His message hit hard. God spoke to me right there and called me to my knees for all of my sins. I prayed to receive Christ, and He turned my life completely around.

"When I called my mom to tell her what I'd done, she sounded skeptical but supportive. Then my grades improved, and I started making new friends. During my senior year I felt a call into the ministry. My major had been in communi-cations, so those classes put me on track for seminary. Anyway, I got my master's while doing my biblical studies, and now I plan to work on my doctorate while ministering to the youth at Abundant Grace."

Hanna found herself feeling warm and smiling, from the inside out. God was so good, and both of them were living proof. "How's your mom and family?"

"Great. She's now a Christian and so are my younger brother and sister. They're all active in a church on the south-west part of town. In fact, Mom is about to remarry."

"What a wonderful testimony. I bet she's proud," Hanna replied softly. She started to ask him why he had never mar-ried but thought better of it.

The hostess seated them and took their drink orders. Mark studied the menu, but she studied him while pretending to be engrossed in the description of entrees. He definitely had matured, both physically and spiritually. Still, she wished he didn't look so incredibly handsome.

Time had only sharpened his good looks. His deep brown eyes with little flecks of gold were his best features. When he glanced up at her, they seemed to penetrate through her—but they'd always had that effect.

Mark appeared to relax and his speech came easier. Hanna wondered about his style of preaching and the way he would deliver a message to the youth. Most likely, he'd do a tremen-dous job. His past certainly put him on the same common ground as many teenagers; then, of course, hers did, too.

So Mark found Christ at a college rally. She had been invited to the same type of meetings, but she had always refused. Maybe her life would have started down the right path sooner if she'd attended Christian gatherings. Instead, she wasted a few more years wandering around without the Lord.

"Are you ready to order?" the waitress asked, taking out her pad and pen.

Mark gave Hanna a questioning glance and she nodded. His manners had certainly improved since high school.

"Okay, your turn," he said to Hanna, once the waitress had taken their orders. "Your story has to be more interesting than mine."

You mean because my attitude is changed, and I'm not over a hundred pounds overweight? a part of her wanted to ask, but she bit her tongue.

"Not really," Hanna replied. "I majored in music at Baylor and received my master's in their program. Once I graduated, I took a teaching position at Pine Forest High School. Believe me, I was pathetic, mainly because I didn't know the Lord. I had a horrible time with the students, and they had no respect for me. Unfortunately, I subjected them to my sarcasm and negative attitude. My biggest problem was my suspicions that they were making fun of me—but in reality they didn't care how I looked." She paused and looked at him curiously. "Are you sure you want to hear this?"

"Absolutely, every word."

She took a deep breath and continued. "Well, one Friday night, the latter part of September, I took all my troubles to McDonald's. Eating had always been my way to escape whatever bothered me. What I didn't realize is that I had turned to food as my savior. It solved all of the misery plaguing me, or at least I thought so. Anyway, the restaurant overflowed with people, and I had to share a table with another young woman. She began to talk to me about Jesus." Hanna shook her head. "The last thing I wanted to hear. Naturally, I ignored her. When she finished her meal, she handed me a gospel tract before she left. For some reason, I didn't toss it into the trash. I took it home and read it. I couldn't believe God actually loved me when I thoroughly despised myself, so I pulled a Bible out of the top of my closet and began reading it from the beginning. Pretty soon, I found myself engrossed with the history of the Jewish people and how God loved them despite their stubborn streak. On Sunday morning, I decided to visit Abundant Grace Church, mainly because the gospel tract had its name stamped on it. There God touched me, and I surrendered my life to Him."

"How remarkable," Mark murmured. "Not everyone can claim they found Jesus at a McDonald's on a Friday night."

Hanna laughed. "True. And the girl who gave me the pamphlet? Now she is one of my best assistants with the youth choir."

Mark paused as though reflecting on all of her words. "Hanna, that's only part of your story. What motivated you to lose the weight?"

Hanna took a drink of her water. "I was at a Christian bookstore looking for something to help me with a boy in my school choir—who is now one of the leaders in our youth group. I spotted a book on eating disorders and felt compelled to buy it. All the pain and suffering I had ever experienced leaped out at me in black and white. It hit me so hard that I became angry, but God used it to convict me of my eating problems." She sighed, remembering the old Hanna.

"Well, God showed me that my size had nothing to do with whether people liked me or not. He loved me unconditionally, but I was guilty of putting food above Him and breaking the first commandment: 'You shall have no other gods before Me.' So, I prayed for guidance, got a complete physical checkup, and discovered that with eating healthy and exercising, the weight came off. That's when God opened my eyes to see the world is full of large people—beautiful, loving creations of God—and what attracts them is a heart molded after Him. So I began teaching weight-management classes."

"How long did it take, losing the weight, I mean?" His soft tone put her at ease. Strange, she had worried he might be disgusted by her admission to an eating disorder.

"Sixteen and a half months."

"Wow, Hanna, you are a very determined woman. Pastor Jacobs told me that your weight-management class is very successful."

"Well, I'm simply allowing God to use me through my own experiences," she replied. "When we first seek a relationship with Him, then He helps us with our imperfections."

"So true. Everything about you is beautiful, inside and out."

She felt her heart take an upward surge. But he had always been able to drop compliments. *Don't trust him,* she told herself. *He may be a minister with all the knowledge, but he's still Mark Alexander, the great charmer.*

"Thank you," Hanna stammered, feeling very self-conscious. "Did you want to get started on your questions about the youth before our food arrives?"

❧

Shortly before midnight, Hanna unlocked her apartment and stepped inside. The evening had gone fairly well, certainly better than she anticipated, and definite progress had been made in the area of friendship.

In the professional arena, Mark exhibited a sharp mind and a keen sense of discernment. He truly cared for the students and seemed eager to guide them into a deeper relationship with Jesus. After assessing the evening, Hanna felt she could work alongside him for the sake of the kids.

He confided in her about the parent conference he'd had with Josie Bennett's parents. The situation worried her, due to Josie's past mental history and her increased weight gain.

The young girl hadn't received Christ or found good friends. After three months in a hospital for depression, she appeared better, but her eyes still held a haunting faraway look. Mark shared the couple's suspicions that their daughter was using drugs. According to her father, she showed all the warning signals of chemical abuse. Hanna prayed their fears were false. She felt a special kinship with Josie, because the young girl had become quite heavy, and her size caused many inappropriate remarks from her peers.

As Hanna waited for sleep to come, she remembered her morning jog with Ryan Henderson. She only hoped it went as well as tonight's dinner with Mark, and a slow smile played on her lips as her eyelids fluttered closed.

four

At seven-thirty Hanna's radio switched on to a local Christian station, and she woke to a popular tune. Reaching over to hit the snooze button, she recalled her jogging appointment with Ryan.

Why didn't I make it at nine o'clock? she inwardly moaned. Her dreams, or rather nightmares, had been of Mark—of him preaching to the students and using her past eating disorder as a symbol of the worst sin imaginable.

"Crazy, stupid dreams," she muttered to herself. *Lord, why did You have to bring him back into my life?* she inwardly grumbled, then instantly regretted her thoughts. *Forgive me for being so selfish.* Hanna knew God had a plan for Mark, and she vowed to support him as the new youth minister.

Within minutes, Hanna had pulled on a pair of jogging shorts, a T-shirt, and running shoes. Hurrying out the door, she finger-combed her thick curly hair back into a high ponytail.

While walking briskly between buildings towards the familiar trail, she realized she had forgotten her house key. "Rats!" she cried, mentally berating herself for the many times she misplaced her keys. And the door always locked when it shut. The only extra key lay in her mail slot at the church office. *I'll deal with it later,* she procrastinated, feeling a surge of frustration at her own negligence.

Scanning the path to the exercise trail, she spotted Ryan waiting. He waved and she returned the greeting. With the sun behind him, he resembled a runner featured in a sports magazine, impeccably dressed in a solid white shorts outfit. A matching headband lifted his blond hair off his forehead, and she envisioned his pale blue eyes. *Maybe I should have taken the time to put on makeup,* she mused. Glancing down at her feet, she cringed. *It's time for a new pair of shoes. What have I gotten myself into this time? Oh well, welcome Ryan Henderson to the real me!*

"Hey, pretty lady," Ryan called with a smile. "You're right on time." She thought how different he looked from Mark. Both were handsome men, but Ryan was as fair as Mark was dark.

"Pure luck," Hanna replied, shaking herself from her reverie. "Sleeping in seemed very tempting this morning."

"You could have gotten your rest; I'd have understood," he insisted, but his eyes twinkled. "Although I would have been gravely disappointed."

"How disappointed?" Hanna asked, seizing the opportunity to tease.

"Probably enough to seek counseling."

His words were enough to make her laugh, and for the moment she forgot about her misplaced keys and Mark. She and Ryan stretched out and eased into the three-mile run. As usual, the first mile proved the most grueling, but then their pace fell into an easy rhythm.

"I haven't enjoyed a morning run this much since yesterday," he stated after the first half mile.

"Well, exercising with someone always makes the time go faster," she said. "Did you have a good Friday?"

"Sure did," he replied. "What about you?"

"Great. There's something about Fridays that makes the worst of days seem better."

"I agree. Did you have a nice quiet evening at home?" Ryan asked.

Hanna hesitated. "Actually, I went to dinner."

"Ah, do I have a rival?"

"Rival for what?" she inquired innocently, her heart hammering like a nearby woodpecker.

"Oh, the hand of Miss Hanna Stewart, of course," he said,

with an attempt at seriousness.

"There's probably a dozen in line, but I'll give you consideration." She did enjoy Ryan's personality.

"How many run with you in the mornings?" he questioned in mock annoyance.

"None."

"Good, it narrows the competition."

Hanna listened while Ryan told her about his large family living in San Antonio, and all of his nieces and nephews, who fought for his attention. His love for kids led him to work with teens.

"What about you?" he asked.

Hanna shrugged her shoulders. "There's nothing exciting about me. Your uncle probably told you all there is to know."

"Do your parents live here in Houston?"

"Yes." She smiled. "They live on the southwest side of town."

"Any brothers or sisters?"

Hanna shook her head. "No, I'm the only one."

He gave her a sideways glance. "You don't like to talk about yourself, do you?"

"Not usually," she replied, "until I get to know a person."

"Well, I can arrange that," he said lightly. "Do you have plans for tonight?"

Hanna paused. Should she invent something or simply decline his invitation? But game-playing had never been a part of her character, and she despised deceit. "Not really," she finally said. "I do have papers to grade."

"Would you consider dinner and a movie?"

Never had she experienced two dates in the same weekend.

"I know it's late notice, but I wanted to ask." Ryan's tone was apologetic. "Have I messed up?"

"No," Hanna laughed. "Dinner and a movie would be fine."

"Great, I'll need your address," Ryan said.

"Truthfully, I'd prefer to meet you somewhere," Hanna

said. "We barely know each other, and I'd feel better with those arrangements."

"Of course," he agreed easily. "What about a casual dinner at the Country Wheel and a movie afterwards at the cinema across the street?"

"Sounds great, but there's something else," she began hesitantly. "I don't see R-rated movies. I can't encourage the students to discern between right and wrong if I don't provide a good example."

"No problem at all. In fact, I think you're a very wise lady—looking out for your own safety and honoring the Lord, too. It's refreshing to meet someone with the same values. . . So, is seven-thirty a good time?"

"Are you okay with all of my stipulations?"

"Yes, ma'am. I might feel a little nervous if you decide to bring a bodyguard, but I could handle it."

"Oh, dear," she said in mocked regret. "He doesn't talk much, but he is over seven feet tall."

They exchanged smiles, and for the first time in a long time, Hanna felt very special.

"Do you happen to have a car phone?" she asked meekly, remembering her plight with her keys.

"Yes, I do."

"Could I use it? You see, I locked my keys inside my apartment, and I need to phone the church secretary."

When he lifted his eyebrows and gave her a puzzled look, she continued to explain.

"She lives in the same apartment complex, and she can get me into the church."

Ryan still looked puzzled.

"I have an extra set in my mail slot at church, and the apartment office doesn't open its doors until ten."

He threw his head back and roared while a slow blush rose from her neck to her cheeks. "Maybe you do need a bodyguard," he added.

By the time Hanna contacted the secretary, who had made a run to the local bagel shop, utter embarrassment had set in.

"Can I drive you anywhere?" Ryan had offered. "Do you want to call someone else?"

Hanna shook her head. "No, thanks, really. Her husband said she would be right back. I'll just wait there."

"Well, I don't want to leave you stranded. . ."

"But I'm not," she insisted. "You go do whatever you have planned, and I'll see you tonight."

"Wish I didn't have hospital rounds this morning," he admitted.

Hanna flashed him a warm smile. "I am perfectly fine, and I'm going right now." She turned and jogged toward the apartment complex without giving him a chance to reply.

Humiliation seeped from every inch of her. *What a lame-brain*, she scolded herself. *Next time I'm wearing those keys around my neck.*

Within the hour she was inside her apartment, sweaty, hungry, and still feeling very foolish. She shrugged her shoulders at the image in her bedroom mirror. Her hair hung in damp ringlets, and somewhere along the way she'd rubbed a huge dirt smudge across her forehead. She began to laugh. It looked like war paint.

"Oh well," Hanna laughed out loud. "There's nothing I can do about it now." She set about doing her least favorite Saturday morning chore—the laundry.

A few hours later, she dumped a load of towels on her unmade bed and hurried through her apartment to pull another load from the washer. As she began tossing the wet clothes into the dryer, the phone rang. Snatching up the portable, she continued working furiously.

"Hello?"

"I bet you're washing clothes," her father said.

Hanna grinned into the receiver. "Yes, I am, and how are you this morning?"

"Real good, honey. . . I know I sound like a meddling father, but I wondered about your dinner with Mark."

"Oh, Daddy, everything went well. We were both nervous, and there were a few awkward moments, but dinner passed pleasantly."

"Good. Do you think you'll be able to work with him?"

"Yeah. . .I think so."

"Has he changed much? I mean, I should hope so."

Hanna laughed. "You would be impressed. He has a beautiful testimony, which I hope he shares with the youth. The only thing that resembles the old Mark Alexander is his physical appearance."

"I'm so pleased. Believe me, I worried about you all evening. Your mother told me not to call, but I couldn't wait any longer."

"I'm just fine. He and I discussed the students and the upcoming mission trip. In fact, we scheduled a meeting for Monday afternoon to continue our talk."

"Do you have time to tell me what changed his life?"

"Sure. It's rather sad. Right after graduation. . ."

After Hanna finished the conversation with her dad, she hung up the phone and finished tending to the laundry. As she had retold Mark's story, it meant more to her than the previous evening. Losing his father after high school graduation must have devastated the whole family. Mr. Alexander didn't hold any father- or husband-of-the-year awards, especially with his alcohol problem, and she had heard he abused them all. But he was their husband and father.

Strangely enough, Mark had found the Lord before Hanna. For sure both of them had reached the bottom of their own worlds before they turned to God. Certainly the years had been good to him; he looked even more handsome than she remembered. Recalling how he enjoyed female attention, she was amazed he hadn't married. "God hasn't put the right girl in my path," Mark had repeated at dinner.

Hanna felt her heart take a little flip. The old feelings had come back to haunt her, and she didn't dare let it show. The two would be spending a lot of time together. And with the upcoming mission trip, she simply must keep her emotions in check.

Perhaps tonight's dinner with Ryan Henderson was the perfect diversion. Except she questioned whether she had done the right thing by accepting the dinner and movie invitation when her heart still carried a flicker of lost love for Mark Alexander.

five

Late that afternoon Hanna answered her doorbell to find a dozen long-stemmed red roses delivered by one of her students. She thanked him and eagerly took the box inside her apartment to privately savor the unveiling. Believing they were from her father, but hoping they were from Mark, she tore open the tiny envelope. The card read: "Looking forward to dinner, Ryan."

Surprised but with a twinge of disappointment, she opened the box. The beauty of the roses enticed her to inhale their sweet fragrance. "They *are* lovely," she murmured, breathing in the fresh scent again. *And very thoughtful, even if a bit premature.*

Hanna tenderly perused each rose and petal. This was a first, for she had never received flowers from an admirer before, other than her father. She must be sure to thank Ryan properly.

After painstakingly arranging the roses, she positioned them on the corner of the piano. The effect of the deep red against the black grand proved stunning. She pulled out a stem and laid it across the ivory and ebony keys. Smiling to herself, she retrieved her camera and snapped a picture. She didn't intend to watch them fade and die without a reminder of their splendor.

With mixed emotions, she realized Ryan could have easily obtained her address from the apartment complex. Rereading the card, a worried frown swept across her face. *He certainly doesn't waste time*, she thought. A flutter of doubt about the evening's plans needled her. *If Ryan is interested in me, he will have to slow down a bit.*

Four outfits later, Hanna emerged from the apartment dressed in a royal blue silk pantsuit and drove to the restaurant where Ryan planned to meet her. She had decided not to question him about sending flowers but merely thank him, unless he said or did something that made her feel uncomfortable. As he walked toward her, she noted the way he carried himself—confident, but not the least bit ostentatious. He wore a fashionable green and navy plaid knit shirt and perfectly creased matching navy slacks.

"You look beautiful," he said simply. A broad smile spread across his boyish face.

"Thank you, and by the way, the flowers are lovely," she replied easily. "It was very thoughtful of you."

"I'm glad you like them. Truthfully, I tried to get them to you earlier, since your day had started out rather. . ."

"Difficult," Hanna finished with a laugh. She shook her head. "Someday I'm going to learn how to keep track of my keys."

"And deny others the privilege of helping you?" he questioned with a wry grin.

"Believe me, there are those who would welcome it."

"Not me," Ryan replied candidly. "I rather enjoyed it. Shall we go inside? I'm starved."

Hanna realized she hadn't eaten since breakfast. A wisp of wind carried the delectable aroma of food from inside the restaurant to her nostrils. "Um, yes. Something smells wonderful."

Unlike the previous night's nervousness, Hanna relaxed and enjoyed Ryan's company. He liked to talk and didn't pressure her with questions, which instantly set her at ease. Obviously he honored her earlier declaration and was giving her time to get to know him.

Leaning into the table, he gave her his complete attention. "I hope I haven't bored you with all of my rambling about work."

"No, not at all," she replied. "I find it fascinating. You must be a powerhouse of energy."

Ryan appeared to consider her words. "Not really. I'm driven by the needs of so many hurting teens, and although the root of their problems is not having a relationship with Jesus Christ, each one still has a personal story. And, Hanna, all their stories are sad." He leaned back in his chair and caught her glance. "I'm talking about my work way too much," he admitted.

"No, you're not," she insisted. "I really do respect your commitment."

"Thanks." He smiled and reached for his water and lemon. "For listening."

A few moments later the waitress scurried off with their plates. Ryan glanced at his watch. "Say, are you ready to go? Our movie starts in twenty minutes."

"Sure," she replied. "What are we going to see?"

He chuckled. "We have a choice between a comedy and a nature film. What sounds best to you?"

"Oh, the comedy." Hanna grinned.

"My thoughts exactly. Just let me get the check and we're off."

Hanna loved the movie, and she enjoyed Ryan's company. Even so, Mark's image filtered in and out of her mind like a subliminal message, and something was missing during the course of the whole evening.

Just before midnight Hanna pulled her car into the covered parking area of her apartment building. Ryan insisted on following her for safety reasons, and he waved good-bye from his vehicle once she unlocked her door. She flipped on the light inside, and her gaze immediately flew to the flowers resting on the piano. Some had opened their delicate, ruby-red petals, as though stretching to make sure she saw them at their finest. Giving in to the urge to breathe in the delicious fragrance, she walked over to the grand, closed her eyes, and inhaled deeply. At that moment, she thought nothing could grace a room more beautifully than roses.

Opening her eyes, Hanna captured her own reflection in the piano's shiny surface and viewed the young woman smiling back at her. The image was blurry, not quite real, and it caused her to honestly assess the evening. She'd had a splendid time with Ryan. Certainly he was a man to be emulated and admired for his dedication to Jesus Christ and his work with teens. And she'd made a good friend.

Examining the opened petals, she remembered how he did everything within his means to convey excellent manners and good taste. She liked him, and he had asked permission to jog with her on Monday.

But he wasn't Mark.

Blinking back a tear, she turned from the piano and allowed the truth to trickle through her. Even after all these years, she still felt very much in love with Mark Alexander. And if she believed in such nonsense, she'd call it a curse. How could she ever get him out of her system? Or did she really want to?

As the tears flowed swiftly down her cheeks, Hanna turned her heart and spirit to her heavenly Father.

Oh, Lord, only You know how I really feel, and I give this all to You. It's wrong to spend time with Ryan when my heart longs for Mark. Or is it? Someday I have to get over this silly schoolgirl crush. Guide my ways, Lord, and help me do only those things that are pleasing to You.

Sensing the late hour and the need to rest before Sunday morning worship, Hanna walked across the room to switch off the light. Just as the room went dark, she saw her telephone answering machine flash red with a message. Her finger pressed the button.

"Hi, Hanna. This is Mark. Thanks again for meeting with me last night. I really enjoyed your company. I didn't know if I would have a chance to speak to you tomorrow, but I need to change our Monday afternoon appointment from three o'clock to five. If this is a problem, leave me a message and we'll arrange another time. Thanks."

What irony, she thought pensively, *that your voice would be the last one I hear tonight. Oh, God, help me not to ruin any good You might have us do by revealing my emotions. It's in Your hands; help me to leave it there.*

❧

Hanna shifted her shoulder purse and waited for Mark to finish his telephone conversation before she entered his office. She had both dreaded and looked forward to the appointment all day. The thought of being alone with him in his office made her feel vulnerable.

She had loved Mark for as long as she could remember, but she was old-fashioned enough to believe he must take the first step toward a relationship—that is, if there ever was supposed to be one.

Didn't you give this all to God? she silently scolded herself. *You have an important job to do, so get over it.*

The phone rang, and Mark's secretary picked it up. "You can go in now." She smiled and replaced the receiver.

"Thanks, and by the way, Nancy, you look great."

"You are so sweet," Nancy whispered. "My husband is thrilled with my weight loss, and the whole family feels better since we started eating more healthy. We've taken on a family walk in the evenings, too. It's provided quality time for all of us to talk about our day."

Hanna felt the warm glow of Nancy's accomplishments. "That is wonderful, and I'm really proud of you. Can I count on you to give a brief testimony at Thursday night's meeting?"

Nancy nodded. "I'd love to, and I'm bringing my mother-in-law. She's interested in the Bible study."

Nancy would never know how her kind words settled the electric sensations in Hanna's stomach. Feeling much more confident with the boost of encouragement, she stepped inside the youth minister's office. He stood to greet her, and she thought his smile could melt the strongest resolve. . .but not hers.

"Thanks for rescheduling our appointment. I hope it didn't inconvenience you." She noticed his hair looked a bit tousled, probably from the light May breeze during lunch. He looked like a playful little boy, and the sight tugged at her senses.

"No, not at all," Hanna replied, seating herself in a stuffed chair facing his desk. "I really needed to stay longer at school, and the extra time allowed me to sort through year-end papers."

"Graduation is in two weeks, right?" When she nodded, he continued. "Preston Taylor invited me to the ceremonies. In fact," he shuffled through several slips of paper by his phone, "I see we have thirty kids from Pine Forest graduating."

"Yes, a good many of them have been with me in choir since I started teaching."

Mark lifted an eyebrow. "Ouch, I bet this will be a tough one for you."

Hanna appreciated his empathy, and smiled. "I plan on bringing a whole box of tissues to graduation."

"Nancy tells me that you have put together a senior breakfast for next Sunday. I saw the program and I'm quite impressed."

"Well, you go ahead and change anything you want," she insisted.

He waved his hands in front of him. "Not on your life. You have all the committees organized and in place. I'm perfectly happy with it as it stands."

"But you will take over officiating?" she asked with a hint of pleading in her voice.

He grinned. "All right. That sounds easy enough." He pulled a yellow legal pad from the corner of his desk, and she recognized it from Friday evening. "Do any of the seniors plan to accompany the mission trip?"

"I believe about half of them have signed up," she replied, pulling out her own notes from her teacher's bag.

"Now where did we leave off on Friday?" Mark asked, his eyes moving down the legal pad. "Oh, here we are. We were talking about including all the youth on the mission trip, not just the choir students."

"You know, the more I think about it, the better I like the idea. They all could help with vacation Bible school, especially since we have no idea how many children in that area might attend. The choir will only be singing at night, and any of the other kids can join in. Your idea sounds great. We do need to decide soon, though, so I can contact the camp and reserve additional cabins."

"Right. I believe I can get everything firmed up by Sunday. Will that be okay?"

"Sure," she replied, while both of them added to their notes. "But this does mean we'll need more chaperons."

"I'll add it to the list." He glanced up. "Can you help me with that? I have no idea who to ask."

"Oh," she replied with mock distress, "I thought you would be much better than me at convincing adults to volunteer."

When Mark lifted an eyebrow and gave his best distressed look, Hanna couldn't help but laugh. "All right, I was just teasing, and I do have some people in mind who might want to come along."

He put down his pencil and leaned back in his chair. "You know, I remember when you used to tease me in chemistry lab, and you were so good at it; I believed every word you said."

"You were quite gullible at times, especially when I cautioned you about mixing chemicals." *I had no idea you remembered those days*, she thought wistfully. The thought carried a strange warmth.

"Well, you were the one who made the As," Mark accused.

"I naturally assumed you knew all the answers."

Giving herself a mental shake, Hanna smiled and wagged her finger at him. "That was your first mistake."

She waited for him to respond, but he said nothing. His brown eyes had a faraway look, and she detected a hint of sadness.

"High school days seem like a lifetime ago," he finally said.

"Well, we were two different people then."

"I hate the way I hurt you." He sighed deeply.

"And I hate the way I acted. But it's all behind us now, remember?"

His brown eyes grew brighter, and she saw the little flecks of gold. "Yes, it's finally settled, and I am so glad we're working together."

"Me, too." For a moment, Hanna thought she might cry— but then he'd ask why, and she'd feel foolish. So, instead she chewed on her lower lip and swallowed the huge lump rising in her throat while her gaze stayed glued to his. The silence between them roared.

At last he tore his stare from her and reached for his pencil. "Why don't you tell me about the camp?"

She inwardly sighed with relief. "Actually, I don't know very much except what I learned from a few telephone calls. It's situated right outside the border town of Progreso, south of Corpus Christi along the Rio Grande River. The camp itself has several bunkhouses, a mess hall, first aid cabin, and a chapel—which is more of a covered pavilion."

"Have the students received any orientation on the people living there?"

"Not yet. They understand the population is largely Hispanic, and many of the people speak both Spanish and English. I believe the majority of children not yet in school speak only their native language, but we do have a Spanish teacher who has offered to join us. With her assistance, the choir has learned a few familiar songs in their language. I've told the kids their main focus will be teaching and aiding in vacation Bible school."

"Great," he said with a nod of his head as he jotted down more notes. "Sure hope you aren't planning to desert me, because I really need your help this summer. Learning all of the students' names is quite a project in itself. And when I consider putting together all the summer activities and the mission trip, well, I'm definitely challenged—more like overwhelmed." He chuckled. "My other churches were not nearly this large. Anyway, I'm hoping you haven't planned a huge summer vacation, but if you have it's okay."

She shook her head at him. "If you hadn't come, who do you think would have been saddled with planning all of the students' summer activities?"

Mark grinned. "I'd hoped you'd see things my way."

Hanna realized then that she could handle her tender feelings for Mark, and he would never find out about the little corner of her heart with his name on it. After all, the kids needed both of them, at least for the summer. Once he became firmly acclimated in his position, she could step back to her choir. Until that time, she faced a huge challenge.

❧

Mark hung up the phone and reached for the notes he'd made during his meeting with Hanna. The scent of her perfume still lingered in the air, and he closed his eyes, envisioning her smile.

You've got it bad, he told himself sternly. *For the first time in your life, a lady has you in the palm of her hand. And she doesn't even know it. Lord, is this why You've brought me to Abundant Grace?*

six

The shrill ring of the phone woke Hanna from a deep sleep. By the time it pierced the silence again, her trembling fingers had fumbled for and found the receiver.

"Hello." She attempted to gather her wits in the darkness, but the haziness between her dream world and reality dulled her senses.

"Miss Stewart," a faint voice whispered.

"Yes." Hanna dug into the recesses of her mind to recognize the girl's voice. "May I ask who's calling?"

"Josie," came the barely audible reply.

Bolting upright, an alarm pealing through her head, Hanna switched on the bedside lamp and brushed the sleep from her eyes. "Josie, what is it? Are you all right?"

"No, I'm not. Miss Stewart. . .I'm scared."

"What's wrong?"

"I. . .I hate myself. I hate the way I look, the way I talk. I hate everything about me." Josie's shaky voice trailed off into silence.

"But you are a wonderful, talented, intelligent girl. There's probably not a girl in the world who hasn't felt like that at one time or another." Deep inside, Hanna sensed something was dreadfully wrong—all of Josie's parents' suspicions and the rumors she had heard from other kids settled on her in a pool of fear.

"I think it's too late, now," Josie whispered.

A creeping dread clutched icy fingers around Hanna's thoughts, and she struggled to remain calm. "It's never too late, honey. Can I pray with you?"

"No," the voice came sharply. "I don't want churchy stuff;

I just want you to talk to me until it's over."

"What's over?" Hanna's heart jolted as though it would leap from her chest.

"My life."

"What do you mean?" *Please, Lord, don't let it be this,* Hanna's spirit silently pleaded.

"I've taken a lot of pills. I'm waiting for it all to be over; I just want to die."

Her pulse hammering, Hanna scrambled from the bed and clicked over to her portable cell phone. She rushed into the kitchen for the telephone book.

"Where are you?"

"In my room."

"What did you take, Josie?" Hanna asked gently, not wanting to frighten the girl into hanging up the phone.

"The pills from the doctor so I wouldn't feel depressed."

"How many did you take?" All the while she spoke, Hanna searched frantically through the directory for the Bennetts' number. She thought the household had two telephone lines.

"The bottle was full." Josie paused. "Miss Stewart, I'm so sleepy. Is this how it ends?"

"I don't know, but I'm coming over to see you."

"Why would you want to see me?" The young girl began to cry, and the audible sound pushed Hanna to search more frantically for the phone number.

"Because I want to help you; because I care about you."

"Just leave me alone and let me die. I don't need any help."

"Yes, you do," Hanna said gently, finally locating the other household line. Her spirit lifted and hope replaced anxiety. "You have parents and friends who love you dearly."

"My parents *have* to love me; no one else does." She paused. "Calling you was a bad idea; I'm going to hang up now."

"No!" Hanna blurted. "Wait a minute. Please, I want to talk

to you, but first I need another blanket. The air conditioning is cold in my apartment. I'll be right back." Hanna pushed the hold button and shakily dialed Josie's parents on her cellular phone. Time raced until finally a man answered.

"Mr. Bennett, this is Hanna Stewart. I have Josie on the other line. She says she has taken a lot of pills."

"Oh, no," he moaned. "Where is she?"

"I believe in her room."

"I'm going to her right now."

"Would you like for me to call an ambulance?"

"Yes, yes, of course."

"The hospital down the street from the church?"

"Yes." Mr. Bennett hung up, and she switched over to his daughter. "Josie? Are you there?"

"Um," she responded listlessly.

"You did the right thing, calling me tonight, because I care for you. And I did the right thing, too. I've phoned your father. I'm sorry to have lied to you, but it was the only way I knew to help you."

"No." Josie's protest sounded weaker than before.

"Yes, and I'm calling an ambulance to take you to the hospital." Hanna heard Mr. Bennett's voice in the background, then he picked up his daughter's phone.

"I've got her now," he said, and the phone clicked.

Completely awake and still trembling, Hanna dialed 911 and explained the emergency at the Bennett home. Once she replaced the receiver, a fervent prayer rose from deep within her. She pled to God for Josie's life and for this tragedy to somehow bring glory to His name. Hanna praised God for using her in the girl's life and prayed for guidance as the young girl's parents dealt with their daughter's unstable mental condition.

Hanna scrambled for her jeans and a T-shirt. Midway through dressing, she realized that as youth pastor, Mark needed to know about the situation. Snatching up the cell phone, she reached for her church staff directory and punched in his number. With every breath she asked God to guard Josie's life.

As Mark's phone rang the third time, her patience dwindled. "Come on, Mark, wake up," she mumbled. "Answer your phone."

"Hello?"

"Mark, this is Hanna. Sorry if I woke you."

"No problem," he replied and yawned. "What's up?"

"Josie Bennett."

"What happened?" Immediately the tone in his voice changed to one of concern.

"She's taken an overdose of pills. I really don't have time to go into it now, but I thought you should know."

"Right," he said hurriedly. "Thanks for calling. Where is she now?"

"At home, but an ambulance is on its way. Do you want to meet me at Northwest General Hospital? It's the one about a mile from the church."

"I'm on my way," he replied. She envisioned him making the same mad scramble for his clothes.

Hanna tossed the phone onto her bed, grabbed her purse and keys, and raced to her car. Whatever happened with Josie tonight, Mr. and Mrs. Bennett shouldn't have to face it alone.

⁂

Mark and Hanna drove into the emergency room parking lot of Northwest General Hospital at precisely the same time. She emerged from her sleek white sports car, grabbed her shoulder bag, and caught his eye. A worried frown creased his forehead.

"How bad do you think she is?" he asked as they walked briskly toward the emergency room entrance.

"I don't know, Mark. I want to believe the ambulance got to her in time."

"What happened?"

"Josie called me crying, and all I could make out was that she felt scared and wanted to die. Her voice sounded thick, and her words were slurred and broken. When I questioned her, she admitted to taking a lot of antidepressants."

"Where'd she get them?" Mark grated, his voice edged with irritation.

"She said the doctor had prescribed them. Anyway I asked her to hold on a minute, then I phoned her parents on my cell phone—the Bennetts have two lines. Well, I explained to Mr. Bennett about Josie, and he rushed to her room. I called 911, and you know the rest."

The automatic glass doors opened for them, and he gave her a reassuring smile. "You were her cry for help," he noted. "It probably saved her life."

Hanna shook her head in disbelief. "I'm not even close to Josie. In fact, she avoids me every chance she gets. Every attempt I've made to befriend her has been met with resentment."

"Maybe that's why she called you," Mark replied thoughtfully. "You kept trying. You didn't give up on her, and she knew you really cared."

Before Hanna could consider his words, they were standing at the ER desk. Glancing around, she didn't see Mr. and Mrs. Bennett.

"We're here for Josie Bennett," Mark informed the receptionist, an older lady with a kind smile.

"She just arrived, sir," the woman said. "In fact, a doctor is with her now."

"And her parents?" Mark continued.

The woman nodded. "They are all back in ER."

"Would you mind letting them know that Hanna Stewart and Mark Alexander are here? We're youth workers from their church."

"Certainly," she agreed. "Why don't you sit down in the meantime?"

Mark thanked the receptionist, and Hanna smiled apprecia-tively. Surveying the busy room, he pointed to a somewhat secluded corner, and she followed.

"Shall we pray?" he asked, once they were seated.

Hanna nodded, and he grasped her hands firmly. His gentle touch felt strangely comforting. "Lord, we come before You tonight for Josie. She's a troubled young woman and desper-ately needs to feel Your love and healing. We pray for wisdom and direction for the doctors and peace for her parents. Guide Hanna and me as we minister to this family. Fill our hearts with Your love and our mouths with the words of comfort that come only from You. In Jesus' precious name. Amen."

He released her hands, and she sensed a bond of under-standing between them.

"I believe she'll be okay," Hanna said softly. "I feel it deep inside."

"I do, too," he replied simply. "This must be horrible for her parents. They've been very worried about her. In fact. . .I think I'll call Pastor Jacobs. They may feel more comfortable talking with him, and besides, he needs to know what has happened, too." Mark glanced about for a phone. "Excuse me a minute."

"Sure," Hanna responded, suddenly feeling very tired and useless.

Her eyes swept across the sea of faces in the waiting room. Some people tried to sleep, some were in obvious discom-fort, and others, like herself, merely waited. A young mother wept quietly while cradling a crying baby, and a pair of teenage boys sat with a friend who held an ice pack over his eye. From the purple and red bruises to his face and the trick-ling of blood from his mouth, Hanna gathered their friend must have been in a fight. A middle-aged couple sat across from her. Neither touched the other; both were deeply engrossed in thought. Only their pain, so evident in the lines burrowed in their faces, gave them any common semblance.

Suddenly aware that her scrutiny might be offensive, her gaze lifted to the pale yellow walls and the nondescript landscapes intended to soothe and comfort. She thought they looked dismal, nothing that would help anyone's heavy heart.

All these hurting people, Lord, Hanna mused. *If I want to hold them all and brush away their tears, then how much more You must feel.* She thought of Josie once more and remembered the despair in her voice. How sad the young girl felt compelled to end her life. How tragic that her problems had become so insurmountable. But Hanna had once felt the same pain; she knew well the hopelessness of feeling no one cared. She also knew only Jesus could fill the void in Josie's life. Hanna took a ragged breath; she must find a way for the young girl to understand how much Jesus loved her.

Hanna watched Mark replace the phone and then join her.

"He's on his way," he said. "I told him what little we knew. I've been thinking. . . Do you suppose she's involved with drugs like her parents suspect?"

"I sure hope not," Hanna replied wearily. "The poor girl has enough problems without adding drug use to the list."

She heard him sigh, and it pricked her attention. "What is it?"

"Oh. . .just wondering if I could have done something to prevent this."

"Like what, Mark? You've only been here a short time," she pointed out.

He gave her a sad smile. "I know, but my ministry is youth, and I want to reach them all."

Without thinking, she rested her hand over his and squeezed gently. "You may have the opportunity to reach her now like never before. God has given both of us another chance."

"I pray so," he said softly, "before it's too late."

Moments later Josie's parents joined them. Mrs. Bennett, an overly slim, frail woman, clung to her tall husband's arm.

She attempted a shaky smile for Hanna and Mark, but still tears flowed unchecked over her pale cheeks. Mr. Bennett patted his wife's hand and greeted the pair.

"Thank you both for coming," he said warmly. "She's going to make it. They've pumped her stomach, but everything looks good."

"Praise God," Hanna murmured.

"I am forever grateful for what you've done tonight," Mrs. Bennett said to Hanna. "If you hadn't been there. . ." The tears flowed swiftly, and she leaned against her husband's shoulder.

"It's all right, dear. Our Josie is in good hands."

"She was always in good hands," Mark added. "And we'll be praying for her."

"Thank you," Mr. Bennett replied, "for everything you both have done for my family. We were going to spend a few minutes in the chapel while waiting to see Josie. Would you like to join us?"

All the while the four walked to the chapel, Hanna felt a strange tugging at her mind. Something felt wrong, terribly wrong.

Why do I feel this way? she asked herself, puzzled and confused. *Josie is going to be all right, and this sweet family has initiated prayer in the chapel.*

But still the thought clung to her.

seven

Hanna pulled on the wide glass doors of Pine Forest High School and stepped inside. She felt achy, tired, and her stomach growled from lack of food. Every inch of her body cried out for sleep and threatened to cease working if it didn't get its way. Her eyes felt like candidates for glue removal, and she had a vague recollection of using eyeliner on her lips. And to top it all, her teacher's bag and purse had somehow gotten tangled between her feet when she exited her car, and she had tripped most ungracefully in front of the principal. The whole thing could have been funny, if not for the circumstances surrounding the all-night vigil.

Glancing into the receptionist's area, she saw Marie bent over the desk with her eyes closed. No doubt she was praying for Josie and her parents. Hanna had phoned her friend at six A.M. to tell her what transpired the evening before. Marie promised to pray and suggested Hanna take the day off.

"I really can't," Hanna had replied. "Today is the last day of school for the seniors, and I have a ton of things to do—besides, I don't want to miss a single minute with my kids."

"You'll be so exhausted that you won't know who's in class," Marie accused with a motherly air.

"You're probably right, but my stubborn side says I have to be there." Hanna wearily trudged down the hallway to her room, dumped an armful of music and student files onto the desk, and returned to the front office.

"You look like you could use one of the cots in the nurse's station," Marie gently chided. "I never did ask how late you stayed at the hospital."

"Um, as a matter of fact, I left around five-thirty this morning."

"And Josie was listed in stable condition then?"

Hanna nodded, and felt a stinging sensation in her eyes. "Yes, and her doctor sounded optimistic. Pastor Jacobs and Mark are still at the hospital with Mr. and Mrs. Bennett."

"Whatever possessed her to attempt suicide—a young girl with her whole life ahead of her?"

Hanna frowned. "She left a note stating she couldn't take people making fun of her weight anymore. I don't know why she called me, because she wouldn't let me get close to her before. But praise God she did."

Marie shook her head in disbelief. "You mean she took all those pills, then called you?"

Hanna nodded grimly.

"And how are Josie's parents?"

"In shock over what has happened to their daughter. I really wish I had been able to get through to her before. . . well, before last night," Hanna said regretfully.

"Honey, you tried. You must have had some kind of impact on her life or she wouldn't have called you."

Hanna remembered Mark making a similar comment.

"Poor little lamb, to face such depression all alone. At least now she will get proper care," Marie continued.

Hanna seized the opportunity to sink into the comfort of a sofa near Marie's desk. "Her parents plan to call her counselor this morning. Of course she will have to be built back up physically before she can work through her mental problems." She rolled her head back, then forward to her chest in an effort to relieve tired muscles. "My head feels like a load of bricks," she softly groaned.

Marie walked around the desk and stepped behind the sofa. "Let me give you one of my famous massages." Not waiting for Hanna to reply, she began to knead the tired muscles in Hanna's neck and shoulders.

"Oh, you are wonderful." Hanna sighed, closing her eyes and allowing herself the luxury of her friend's nimble fingers. "But I shouldn't be sitting here like this."

"How's that?"

Hanna sighed deeply. "Well. . .because it's selfish."

Marie chuckled as she pressed her thumbs into tight shoulder muscles. "Explain it to me, girlfriend, 'cause I'm not connecting."

She wet her lips. "I feel like I let the Bennetts, Pastor, and Mark down by deserting them this morning. I mean, they are all still there at the hospital."

"And what are you doing?"

"Indulging in a massage. . ."

"Correction. You're taking a moment for yourself before you tackle an energetic bunch of high school students."

Hanna grinned despite her horrible frame of mind. "Guess you're right, but I do feel guilty about them staying at the hospital without me."

"Nonsense," the older woman scolded. "How did Mark handle it all?"

She instantly perked up. "Oh, Marie, you should have seen how well he managed things. He said the right things, did the right things. He was a real blessing to the Bennetts." *And to me*, an inward voice admitted.

"Good. I've been praying for him—especially when you told me about his younger days," Marie replied. "Not that I wanted to judge him. . .but I was hopeful that he would do an excellent job with the youth and parents."

"An outstanding job. No need to worry." Long moments passed, and Hanna felt herself giving in to precious sleep.

"Hanna?"

"Hmm."

"Are you falling for Mark all over again?"

Hanna forced a smile. "Why ever would I want to put myself in that predicament again?" But she wondered if her hasty answer gave away her true emotions.

Marie patted her on the shoulder, and in the same instant the telephone rang. "You answered my question," she said with a laugh and hurried to the phone.

Hanna shook her finger at Marie. She felt too tired to protest. A quick glance at her watch told her she didn't have much time before students arrived. "I'd better grab some coffee and put some life into this body," she whispered while her friend tended to the phone. *The kids deserve a perkier music teacher than what I feel. This will definitely be one of those days when I am weak and God is my strength."*

❧

At noon Hanna phoned the hospital for an update and found that Josie had begun responding to treatment. She remembered her devotion from yesterday, Psalm 139, and it brought peace to her spirit:

"For You created my inmost being; You knit me together in my mother's womb. I praise you because I am fearfully and wonderfully made; your works are wonderful, I know that full well. My frame was not hidden from you when I was made in the secret place. When I was woven together in the depths of the earth, your eyes saw my unformed body."

God loves you, Josie, Hanna thought. *You are special to Him, because you are wonderfully made. Thank You, Lord.*

Hanna planned to stop at the hospital right after school. Then from seemingly nowhere, the same uneasiness from the night before rose in her mind. She couldn't figure out why the Bennetts' behavior bothered her. They were good church-going people—regular in attendance and supportive of Josie. But Hanna knew that didn't necessarily mean everything was settled right at home. Problems often hid beneath the surface, and a crack in the family unit could mean a deep lesion somewhere else. In this case, the lesion might well have something to do with Josie.

I'm overreacting, she told herself. *I'm tired and looking for someone to blame. After all, I had a self-esteem problem, and my parents were not at fault.*

Still, the thought persisted, and she couldn't shake it loose.

After a grueling day, Hanna drove to the hospital. Sleepiness pestered her unmercifully, but she simply had to see Josie. For some reason, the young girl had called her after taking the overdose. Hanna felt a strange bonding to the troubled teen and a deep need to cement their relationship. She wondered about Josie's response to Hanna phoning her parents. Would she be hostile and feel her initial trust destroyed?

A part of her also wanted to see the Bennetts so she could dispel the nagging doubts prevailing in her mind. The thoughts seemed to engulf her common sense, making her feel frustrated at herself for thinking they might not be good parents, especially when they appeared so concerned about their daughter.

The clinical smell of the hospital lingered in the long corridor to Josie's room. A grinding ache pounded at Hanna's temples, and her eyes felt like splinters held them open. Even worse, her stomach churned, which often occurred when she attempted to function on a sleep deficit. Shifting her purse onto her shoulder, she took a deep breath before entering the room.

I've got to be cheerful for Josie and her family, she told herself. *And I don't dare cry at the sadness of it all.*

Mr. and Mrs. Bennett, Pastor Jacobs, and Mark were seated near Josie's bed. The pastor and Mark smiled warmly into Hanna's anxious face. They all looked exhausted.

"Our patient is doing much better," the pastor whispered. "But she's very tired."

Hanna walked over to the bed. "Hi, Josie," she said very pleasantly.

The young girl, groggy and on the verge of drifting off to sleep, smiled through closed eyes. "Hi, Miss Stewart."

"Are you feeling better?"

"Yes, ma'am," she replied weakly.

Hanna bent closer. "I'm so glad. You rest now, and I'll come back tomorrow."

Josie's eyes fluttered and opened slightly. "Miss Stewart. . . I'm not mad at you."

Hanna swallowed the hard lump in her throat. "Thank you; that means so much to me." She placed a light kiss on Josie's forehead just as the girl's eyes closed. Reaching for a tissue, Hanna dabbed her nose before turning to the others. "Sorry, I really feel weepy."

"No need to apologize," Mrs. Bennett whispered. "We've cried off and on all day."

Hanna smiled at the woman's understanding. Her worries about the Bennetts must certainly be unfounded. She stared down at Josie. The young girl slept so peacefully, with no visible signs of the war raging inside her. Turning her attention to those around her, Hanna saw the telltale marks of fatigue on all of them. "And how are you all doing? Have you been able to rest?"

Standing, Mrs. Bennett reached across her daughter's bed and grasped Hanna's hand. "Thank you for asking," she said, her words laced with emotion. "Especially when you haven't had a moment to rest yourself. We did doze some, but we wanted to be awake in case she needed us."

"Are you planning to go home and get some sleep tonight?" Hanna asked.

"I'm spending the night here," Mr. Bennett interjected. "I've got vacation days coming, and Linda needs her rest."

The woman started to object, but her husband gently silenced her. "Let me do this for you and Josie. I want to work on my relationship with my daughter. She knows you love her, but I'm not so certain she believes I do."

Mrs. Bennett silently acquiesced, and he placed his arm around her shoulders.

"How long do you think she will be hospitalized?" Hanna

asked. "Or is it too early to speculate on her recovery?"

"Well," he began, "my guess is once she is released from here, she'll spend another four weeks at another facility to work through her problems."

"Is there anything I can do for you?" she continued.

Mr. Bennett shook his head. "I can't think of a thing except to keep Josie in your prayers and visit her when you can."

"Of course," Hanna agreed. "And please tell her that I will be back tomorrow after school." She glanced over at Mark who had been silent. She saw the lines etched across his forehead and around his brown eyes. A smile passed between them, and despite the circumstances, the warmth of his gaze did her heart good. "I believe I'll go on home now," she quietly announced. Jotting down her numbers for home, school, and her cell phone on a slip of paper, she handed it to Mr. Bennett. "Here's where to reach me if you need anything—anything at all."

"We surely will, and thank you for coming this afternoon."

"I think Mark and I are going to leave, too," Pastor Jacobs said. "Can we hold hands for a word of prayer?"

When they finished praying, Pastor Jacobs lingered with the Bennetts, but Mark joined Hanna in the hall.

"You *are* going to get some sleep, right?" he asked, and she heard the concern in his voice.

Hanna laughed lightly. "Yes, no arguing that point." Pausing, she asked, "Do you think Josie will be all right, I mean, really?"

Mark tilted his head thoughtfully. "I believe so—with lots of prayer and support. I believe her counselor plans to stop in tonight. According to the Bennetts, he's a strong Christian, and she likes him. Her parents have been bringing her to him for a while now, because they were concerned about Josie's moodiness."

"Good. I'm praying all of this will bring her closer to the Lord—and to her parents."

"Yeah, she doesn't need any more crises like last night."

The two stood in front of the elevator, but before Mark could push the down button, it opened and Ryan Henderson appeared. He looked polished and perfect, sporting a wide smile.

"Hanna, what are you doing here?" he asked.

"Well, visiting a young friend who went through quite an ordeal last night," she replied, feeling very uncomfortable, for some reason, with both Mark and Ryan standing before her.

"Would her name be Josie?" he inquired.

"Are you her counselor?" she asked in amazement.

He nodded. "I put the pieces together when you weren't at the jogging trail this morning, and then Mr. Bennett called me about his daughter."

Hanna suddenly remembered she hadn't introduced the two men. "I'm so sorry. Ryan, this is Mark Alexander, our youth minister. Mark, this is Ryan Henderson—Josie's counselor."

The two shook hands, but Hanna still felt awkward. Glancing at Mark, she saw an odd look about him—a peculiar glint in his eyes that she hadn't seen before.

"My pleasure," Mark said politely. "The Bennetts speak highly of you."

"Thank you. I imagine we will meet again, especially as we work with Josie," Ryan replied. "Well, if you'll excuse me, I really need to visit with our friend and her family." He flashed another smile in Hanna's direction. "Will I see you in the morning?"

"Sure," she replied much more easily than she truly felt. "I'll be there."

Ryan nodded and headed toward the hall.

Silently, Hanna and Mark rode the elevator down to the hospital's lobby.

"I am so beat," she finally said.

"Me, too. I'm too old to pull all-nighters." He paused. "Actually, I've heard of Ryan Henderson. He has an excellent reputation; I hope he can help Josie." His words sounded choppy and forced, but she contributed it to his lack of sleep.

"The Bennetts seem to believe in him. Of course, she has to want the help," Hanna added.

Mark nodded and sighed deeply. "I should have given him my card. . .in case he needs to contact me."

"I'll pass it along," Hanna offered.

"All right." He reached inside his wallet and produced his business card. "Thanks, Hanna—not just for giving Ryan my card, but for everything you did last night. I would have been lost without your constant encouragement."

She stole a sideways glance at him, and he met her gaze. His eyes were red and puffy, and she guessed hers looked the same. "Whatever I did last night was out of love and concern for everyone involved."

"That's my girl," he said softly. "Promise me you are going home to bed."

"I promise." The look he gave her sent a tingling from her head to her toes.

&

Mark slid into his car seat and leaned his head back. He could easily fall asleep right there, but as tired as he felt, certain things plagued his mind and heart.

Lord, I know I've thanked You before, but again I praise Your name for bringing Josie and her family through this crisis. Guide us all as we nudge her toward You. And thank You for. . .

His thoughts turned full circle to Hanna—sweet, lovely Hanna, who seemed to be occupying a lot of his thoughts lately. Her beauty glowed from the inside out. He already longed to see again those tear-shaped eyes full of expression and tenderness that somehow comforted and lifted him at the same time. Thinking about their dinner together, he recalled seeing his reflection in those violet pools. Something happened to him that momentous night. It seemed as though the

Lord shook him senseless and told him she was the one. . . Surely he couldn't be in love after so short a time. . .but hadn't he known her a lifetime?

He remembered the pang of jealousy he felt a few minutes ago, a totally foreign sensation. Never, absolutely never had he experienced jealousy over a woman. Before he found the Lord, his relationship with women had been more of a game, nothing serious. Afterward, he had no desire to seek out a relationship, only to do God's will.

Forgive me, Lord, I know envy is a sin. But he didn't want another man in Hanna's life—and now he felt convicted of selfishness!

"Whew," he said out loud. *What have I gotten myself into?* Mark shook his head. If he didn't feel so bone-tired, he'd laugh. *Mark Alexander and Hanna Stewart. Who would have ever thought of them together?*

Starting up the engine, he pulled from the parking lot, grinning like he'd just found a bag of chocolate-covered peanuts. Then, glancing up at the hospital, he suddenly remembered bits and pieces of a conversation he'd overheard earlier. He'd been dozing in a chair, and Pastor Jacobs was out of the room.

"Don't you think you're overdoing it a bit, dear?" Mr. Bennett asked his wife while Mark drifted between the haze of sleep and wakefulness.

"Who are you to criticize?" she retorted.

"Her father," he replied calmly. "And I'd advise you to keep your voice down."

Mark didn't like the caustic implication of their words. At first it surprised him, now it confused and irritated him. Had he been duped by the Bennetts; for that matter, had they all been fooled?

eight

"Josie is being released today," Ryan said nearly three weeks later as he and Hanna jogged past the first mile marker. They had met nearly every morning since that first Saturday. He had seemed unusually quiet this morning, and now she understood why.

"Isn't it a bit premature?" she asked. Already, the warm, humid temperature had caused a trickle of perspiration to drip down her back. "She does seem much happier, but I didn't realize she was ready to go home."

"Appears to be so," he said impassively.

"Don't you think she's better?" Hanna felt a twinge of alarm.

"Maybe."

Ryan's noncommittal response both shocked and filled her with misgivings. "Obviously, you don't think so," she pointed out.

"I don't have the final word," he replied in the same flat tone. "The attending psychiatrist consults me, but he's responsible for the final decision. And he's been her doctor for the past two years."

They jogged for the next half-mile in utter silence. A hint of a breeze picked up the loose tendrils of damp hair around Hanna's face and cooled her slightly. Although it refreshed her, her worried frown drove away any semblance of a pleasant morning. Deep in thought, she wondered what had transpired with Josie's therapy. Just yesterday, Linda Bennett had phoned Mark singing praises about Ryan's counseling and her daughter's steady progress. What could have happened in the last twenty-four hours to change things?

"Will you tell me what's going on?" she finally asked. Then

73

she considered the confidentiality of his patient-counselor relationship with Josie. "Or can't you?"

"Oh, I can tell you some of it," he stated grimly. "Her parents have decided she no longer needs hospitalization or my counseling."

Hanna stopped in her stride. "What? You're kidding! She overdosed less than three weeks ago!"

Turning, Ryan retraced the steps he'd taken beyond her. "And today she goes home. I'm 'relieved' of my responsibilities," he said tersely.

"Can they do that, legally, I mean?"

"She has a new therapist."

Her mouth gaped in disbelief. Confusion and frustration caused a shiver to race through her sweat-laden body. "I can't believe that. Why ever would they dismiss you just when it seems the counseling is actually starting to help?"

Ryan chuckled bitterly. "I'm sure you will hear about this, but I'd rather tell you myself. The Bennetts believe Josie is having romantic delusions about me, which is totally absurd. I think I'd be the first to recognize a patient's inappropriate attitude toward me."

"I don't believe this. What will the change do to Josie's mental health?"

He sighed deeply. "Probably put her back to square one. I tried to tell them that it takes time for a counselor to build up trust with a patient, but they believe I'm doing more harm than good."

Hanna couldn't believe the ludicrousness of the Bennetts' decision—unless, of course, they were correct. "And you're sure Josie isn't infatuated with you?"

"Not in the least," he stated firmly. "We were actually getting to the root of many things."

Hanna shook her head in an effort to dispel the anger. "Are you going to call Mark?"

"Already have before I came here this morning. Only I

didn't tell him why I had been dismissed, so, please, don't say anything."

"Of course," she replied. "Guess all we can do is pray and hope the new therapist is able to get to the root of her problems."

"I agree," he stated, "because I'm really worried about her."

Bewildered and feeling totally helpless, Hanna couldn't help but question why. Josie's parents had made their decision. It made no sense for them to purposely halt their daughter's counseling with Ryan unless. . . Now she wondered about her earlier assessment of the Bennetts. Maybe she shouldn't have been so quick to abandon her apprehension.

❧

Normally Hanna allowed herself the luxury of a long, leisurely shower. She planned her mornings that way: a long quiet time with God, a long run, and a long shower. But this morning she rushed through her routine, anxious to talk to Mark and equally impatient to get some answers. Pure anger raced through her veins, and the more the water washed over her, the more upset she became at the whole situation.

Remembering the Bennetts' explanation of why they ended Josie's therapy infuriated her. Only three weeks had passed since the suicide attempt, and in Hanna's opinion, they were throwing the girl to the wolves. Granted, Ryan was an extremely handsome man, charming, and witty. And she could see how a young girl might easily misinterpret his interest in her wellbeing as something romantic, but Ryan was a Christian professional with an outstanding reputation. Certainly he would have detected a teenage girl's infatuation? She wanted to believe the Bennetts had good reasons for their actions. But were those reasons in Josie's best interests or theirs? And why?

Slow down, she told herself. *You don't have all the facts, and you may not get them, either. You're not Josie's parents, or a trained professional, or for that matter God.* This realization pulled her senses to a halt. *But I care about her*, she stubbornly insisted. *Don't I have a right to help? Don't I have a right to know the truth?* Silence slammed her heart to a standstill.

Uttering a prayer for understanding, Hanna inhaled deeply and humbly asked her heavenly Father for guidance and wisdom.

&

Hanna walked into Mark's office determined to follow through with the observations she had made. Usually she headed straight for her office, since her role with the church's youth expanded during the summer months, but not this morning. Feeling a bit shaky and not sure if her trepidation was due to her mission or her ever mounting emotions for him, she forced a nervous smile. Hopefully she wouldn't break down and cry in front of him, which she normally did when upset and confused. Crying would completely embarrass her.

Mark's secretary looked deeply engrossed as she shuffled through student applications for the mission trip. Hanna stood for several seconds before the woman noticed her. "Hi, Nancy," she finally greeted.

The woman flashed a warm smile, and it helped to soothe Hanna's anxiety. "Oh my, I didn't see you standing there. Hi. Are you wanting to see Mark?"

"Yes, is he busy?"

"Not any more than usual. Let me ask him."

Hanna dug her fingers tightly into her palms while Nancy spoke to him.

"Go on in," Nancy said, then she lowered her voice. "He's not in a very good mood."

Hanna cringed; what timing. Maybe she should make an excuse and forget it all until another time. "Thanks," she whispered. "I think I'll be quick."

"Oh, he'll be fine once he sees you," Nancy teased.

Hanna lifted an eyebrow questioningly.

"Nothing, I'm just making an observation," Nancy replied

and turned her attention to the papers before her.

Carefully closing the glass door behind her, Hanna studied Mark's face. He looked much older with lines furrowing around his eyes, and they brought back memories of the night Josie overdosed. While chewing on the top of a pen, he turned the page of the Bible before him. Inwardly sighing, Hanna definitely felt like an intruder.

"I'm sorry, Mark, looks like I'm interrupting you," she said hastily. "I'll check back with you later." Reaching for the doorknob, she turned to leave for her own office down the hall, but his voice stopped her.

"No," he barked.

Hanna jumped at his tone.

"Oh, great. I mean, please don't leave."

She saw a look of pleading cloud his normally bright eyes. Silently, she slipped into a chair in front of his desk.

"How did you know I needed to see you?" he asked without reservation, running his fingers through his black hair. "I've been praying for you to come right through this door."

She gave him a half smile. "I guess we need to talk."

"From the look your face, I gather it's about the same topic."

Hanna shifted uncomfortably, not sure how to put her thoughts into words. She glanced down at her hands folded neatly in her lap. *Oh, Lord, help me to be factual and not ramble on.*

"I know Ryan phoned you this morning," she began. "He told me what happened."

Mark nodded slowly. "Since then, Mr. Bennett has called, too, and I'm sure he will contact you before the morning is through."

Hanna paused, her heart pounding wildly. "So, what did he tell you?"

Mark closed his Bible and hesitated before replying. "That he and Mrs. Bennett have decided to take Josie home today and to terminate Ryan as their daughter's counselor."

"Did he give you a reason why?"

Mark leaned back into his chair and drummed his pen on the desk. "Yeah. He said they believe she no longer needs hospitalization. They also think she is infatuated with Ryan."

Hanna gazed into his brown eyes and gave him a faint smile. "Frankly, I don't know what to think. In one breath, I'm glad she's made such excellent progress, and in the next, I question their decision to change therapists."

He shook his head as though agitated. "Well, I want to respect their position as her parents and believe they have prayed about what is best for Josie, but other things have really bothered me."

Hanna felt a deep sinking in her spirit—the same pestering thoughts about the Bennetts, the reason why she had been led to talk to Mark this morning. She had to ask. "What other things?"

He stood and walked to a window overlooking a grove of towering pines. The trees swayed back and forth like tall, skinny old men. Hanna tore her eyes from the sight and focused on Mark. She believed he wrestled with his words, and as difficult as it was for her, she waited patiently.

"I asked if I could stop by and see her and possibly bring you, but Mr. Bennett prefers that you and I not visit Josie. He feels that his daughter shouldn't be talking to anyone except her new therapist. It's a 'personal' decision based on a discussion with his wife and Josie's psychiatrist." Mark faced her, his handsome features rigid and his eyes radiating fire. "I know for a fact her doctor is a Christian. Now, what damage could you or I do?"

Hanna sat glued to the chair. Her thoughts spun, and her apprehension about the Bennetts clamored about her mind like a myriad of ringing bells. She raised her eyes to meet his, and she realized the time for truth had arrived.

"Mark." She swallowed, then breathed a silent prayer. "You and I both know prayers and love are what Josie needs from those who care about her. But I do want to say something—call it an inkling or a feeling or whatever." She took a deep breath and wet her lips. "Like you, I don't want to judge the Bennetts; that's wrong, but at the same time, I wonder about the whole family situation."

She stood and began pacing the floor. "I realize I may sometimes have these weird premonitions, but ever since the night Josie overdosed, I've suspected something amiss." She stopped in the middle of the room and stared into his eyes. "And I have nothing solid to base it on."

Silence filled the room for an endless moment.

"I've had the same feeling," he said softly at last. "Especially since I overheard a conversation the day Pastor Jacobs and I stayed at the hospital. It has me baffled."

She ceased pacing and stared at him. "What did you hear?"

"Frankly, I hesitate to repeat part of a conversation, but I'm assuming what you and I discuss stays within this office." Mark paused until she gave a consenting nod. "Well, Pastor Jacobs had stepped from the room, and I was half asleep when I heard Mr. and Mrs. Bennett talking. He asked her if she was overdoing it a bit, and she responded by asking him who he was to criticize. Then he told her to keep her voice down. I know it sounds innocent enough, but at all the other times, the two were saying and doing all the loving, good, parent things. I'm probably overreacting, but maybe not. I wonder."

"Wonder what?" Hanna asked.

"If Ryan could have been on the verge of getting to the core of Josie's problems, and her parents reacted out of fear."

Hanna listened intently. He seemed ashamed of his words, as if speaking them made him a lesser man of God.

"Let's stop right now and pray," he said firmly. "God is in control here, and He loves Josie more than you or I ever could. We have to believe all of this is working toward her mental healing, her acceptance of Jesus as her Savior. It's easy for us to see one side of the picture, and for me to make hasty conclusions. Mr. Bennett assured me that the new therapist is a believer."

Hanna felt the chilly air conditioning and she wrapped her arms about her. "I'm ashamed of my thoughts and suspicions about the Bennetts, and I know it's because I see so much of the old me in Josie."

Mark gave her a sad smile. "Let's pray." They bowed their heads and he began. "Heavenly Father, we praise Your name and Your infinite wisdom. This morning we come to You with heavy hearts for our dear little sister Josie and her family. We want what is best for them, and we confess we haven't loved this family as You have instructed us. Forgive our foolish hearts, for we realize only You can meet their needs and heal their problems. We ask that You be with her psychiatrist and therapist as they prayerfully work together to help the Bennett family. And we also ask You to give Ryan peace and contentment in this difficult time. We want Your will, Lord, and even if we don't understand it, we accept it. Guide us in Your truths. All these things we ask in Your precious Son's name, Jesus. Amen."

"Amen," Hanna repeated.

"It will all work out," Mark assured her. "We simply need faith and trust—just like we tell the kids."

Hanna realized she felt closer to Mark than ever before. He was her friend in Christ. They had shared a tragic experience with Josie's overdose, and they had rejoiced in the news of her recovery. It proved God's provision for His children and the ever-increasing need to trust and pray without ceasing. More importantly, they needed faith in the Almighty Father's provision.

❧

At the end of the day, Hanna sat at her kitchen table and nursed a cup of hot coffee. Although the outside temperatures soared, she felt cold and drained. The day had been grueling and unrelenting—from learning about Josie's hospital release, to an irate father complaining about his son needing a physical before the mission trip, to a single mom worried about the cost of financing the youth summer activities. All required patience, understanding, time, and prayer. And she felt exhausted, mentally and otherwise.

When the phone rang, she decided to let the answering machine get it, but the sound of Mark's voice changed her mind.

"Yes, Mark, I'm here," she said, clicking off the machine.

"Hi. How are you doing?"

"Honestly? Hmm, I've had better days."

"Me, too." Mark hesitated. "Could I interest you in meeting me for dinner? I'd sure like the company."

Hanna contemplated the matter. She really had intended to practice piano, but an invitation from Mark sounded much better. "Okay, sure. What did you have in mind?"

"Nothing fancy," he said apologetically.

"Good, 'cause I'm in jeans and a T-shirt."

"What about the Southern Spoon? I could go for some home cookin'."

She laughed. "Yeah, it's probably good for the soul."

"I've heard they have biblical alphabet soup."

She laughed again. "What's the difference between biblical and regular alphabet soup?"

"It's all in Greek and Hebrew."

"Oh, that's terrible," Hanna groaned.

"Will you still meet me for dinner?" he asked meekly.

"I suppose," she deliberately faltered. "But only if you promise to work on your jokes."

"I'm crushed," he replied in a hurt tone. "I'd saved that one special for you."

"And I appreciate the effort, but you can always try again."

He chuckled, and the light, relaxed sound lifted her spirits. "How soon could you be ready?"

"I'll be at the Southern Spoon in thirty minutes."

"Great. You're a lifesaver, Hanna. I'll see you in a little bit."

Suddenly, Hanna found she had new energy.

nine

"I give up on telling you jokes," Mark declared, throwing his hands up in feigned annoyance. "You obviously don't have a sense of humor."

"Oh, yes, I do," Hanna insisted with a giggle. "I just haven't heard anything funny yet."

"Guess I'll have to go back to being intellectual," he sighed.

She broke into laughter. "Now, that is funny."

Mark scowled and shielded his face with the menu. Pretending to study the Southern Spoon's list of entrees, he said, "The cuisine prepared at this excellent establishment deems it difficult to maintain the composure necessary to select the. . ."

"Don't look now, Professor," Hanna whispered, leaning into the table and interrupting his dissertation, "but we are about to be invaded by Abundant Grace's youth group, a big bunch of them."

His eyes flew wide and a huge grin spread across his features. "Hey, those *are* our kids," he commented, as the dozen or so students migrated to Mark and Hanna's table.

Preston Taylor led the group, holding hands with a pert little blond Hanna recognized as Lorie. He lifted his chin in a silent greeting, while the rest behind him whooped and hollered.

"And there's the leader of the pack," she whispered to Mark.

"A whole lot of truth in that statement," he chuckled.

Before she had time to respond, the students had descended upon them.

"Hi," Mark and Hanna chorused.

"Hey to you," Preston replied in his normal, good-natured

tone. "So you two are hangin' out?"

"Sort of," Mark responded. "What are all of you up to?"

"Looking for someone to buy us dinner," Preston said, and a burst of laughter exploded from the students.

"Keep looking," Mark announced dryly. "I'm too broke to feed an army."

"Man, you really let me down." Preston looked dejected and turned his attention to Hanna. "Miss Stewart, is Pastor Mark treating you right? 'Cause if he isn't, I'll take him outside and teach him some manners."

"Well," Hanna began, winking at the man seated across from her, "he did force me to listen to some bad jokes."

"That does it," Preston shook his blond head, his blue eyes dancing. "His jokes are the worst, right, guys?" He roused the attention of the others. "Last Sunday night he took us to his apartment to watch videos and have pizza, then told jokes the entire time. We were hurtin'."

"I'm sorry," Hanna said sympathetically. "I know exactly how you feel."

Preston continued his harassment of Mark. "Do you see any reason why we shouldn't put him out of his misery?"

She put her hand up in front of Preston in defense of the youth minister. "But he does have some good qualities."

"Oh, no. I can't believe a lady is protecting him," Preston moaned. "Okay, give me one."

Hanna placed her finger to her lips thoughtfully.

"Beep, time's up." Preston smiled, then bent to put his arm around Mark's shoulders. "He really is a good guy. After all, he puts up with us."

"Amen," Mark said, with a wry smile. "That should be worth something."

Ignoring his clip, Preston went on. "It's good to see you two together. I think ya'll look great—real cozy like. Hope it lasts."

Hanna felt a slow rise of warmth and color creep up her

neck and into her cheeks. If she could have hushed the teen with a single glance, she gladly would have, but her disapproval would only increase the teasing. After having him in choir for four years, she knew that much about Preston Taylor's habits.

"Preston," Lorie admonished, "you're embarrassing Miss Stewart. Don't pay any attention to him," she instructed Hanna, then took on a serious tone. "I keep wondering about Josie. How is she doing?"

Thankful for the change in topic, Hanna quickly replied, "She may have gone home from the hospital today."

The news about Josie seized all the students' attention.

"Maybe we could go see her," one of the other girls said.

Hanna tilted her head. "Um, not just yet," she gently advised, remembering her late-afternoon call from Mr. Bennett with a request not to contact his daughter. Even so, the kids might be able to visit her later. "Josie may need a couple of days to get used to home again."

"You're right," Lorie said. "And we probably should call her parents first anyway—find out a good time to visit."

Hanna nodded.

"We could say we wanted to talk to her about the mission trip. That way she wouldn't feel uncomfortable," Lorie suggested, glancing up at Preston questioningly.

"Yeah, I'll go," he replied, then turned his attention back to Mark and Hanna. "Well, talking to you has been great, but we'd better get a table before the management throws us out."

Mark shook his hand. "Thanks for stopping by. We love you guys."

"Yeah, we love you, too." Preston grinned. "And take care of Miss Stewart. She's the best."

As the group disappeared to a set of corner tables, Hanna cringed at the teen's parting remark. Oh, Preston's words were innocent enough, and she appreciated his loyalty and fondness for her, but what if someone could see her growing love for Mark?

Hanna glanced up and found Mark studying her. His smile brought another telltale blush to her face, and she instantly sought refuge behind her menu.

"Sorry the kids embarrassed you," he said softly.

"Oh, it's all right." She avoided his eyes, wishing she could give Preston a piece of her mind.

"But Preston's right," he added. "You are the best, and I praise God for putting you into my life again."

Her stomach fluttered as hope raced through her. Did she dare think he cared for her—or was she clutching at only a faint semblance of real love?

"Thank you," Hanna managed, trying to calm her pounding heart. She struggled to think of something casual to say. As if on cue, a tall waiter towered over their table.

"Have you decided what you'd like?" he asked pleasantly. "Or are you interested in the special?"

Although she welcomed the diversion, her heart sank; she had wanted to savor the tender moment for as long as possible.

Mark peered at her, the little gold flecks in his eyes sparkling. "Do you know what you want?"

What a leading question, she thought with an inward smile. *Unfortunately, I know what I want all too well.* Looking up at the waiter, she asked innocently, "Do you have alphabet soup?"

Mark choked back his laughter as he ordered his meal.

The waiter brought them a basket of cornbread and biscuits with two huge glasses of iced tea, and their conversation moved to the youth and their activities. When Hanna and Mark had finished their meals, they walked slowly toward their cars.

Thank You, God, for ending this hectic day with such a blessing, she thought as gratefulness embraced her emotions. *I pray I haven't read anything into Mark's words that are not from You. I want so much for things to work out between us, but this may not be in Your plan. And my heart's desire is to be obedient to You, and You alone.*

She looked up at the cascade of stars filling the navy blue sky.

"Beautiful night," Mark remarked. "When I was a kid, my grandmother told me the stars were the angels lighting candles for Jesus."

Hanna smiled and stared wistfully into the sky. "What a sweet story. I'll have to remember it. Is your grandmother still living?"

"No, she passed away a few years ago," he replied. "After I surrendered my life to Jesus, she told me she had prayed for me every day."

"Shows you the power of prayer."

"And God's perfect timing."

Silently they stood beside her car. Hanna didn't know what else to say, so she dug through her shoulder bag for her keys. Fortunately, she was able to wrap her fingers around them without much trouble.

"Thanks for dinner," she said. "I had a great time."

"Me, too. Guess I'll see you tomorrow. If you have time after lunch, I'd like to finalize the mission trip."

"Sure. I have a few students who haven't returned their physical forms yet, so I'll contact them in the morning."

"Good." He sighed. "And thanks for joining me for dinner. I had a great time, even if the kids did show up."

Hanna flashed him a shadowed smile and reached for the door handle, dropping her keys in the process. Hearing the ping as they hit the cement, she groaned. "I can't believe I did that."

They both knelt on the pavement between Hanna's car and a van parked close beside hers. She smelled his cologne— tantalizing and tempting.

"They can't be far," she said, patting the parking lot around her knees, exasperated. "I heard them hit."

"So did I." Mark searched the dark area below him for the keys. "Maybe they landed under the car."

Both reached under the driver's side, but Hanna found the keys a quick second before Mark's hand closed over hers.

"I've got them," she breathed, intensely aware of his touch.

"And I've got you," he whispered.

As her fingers curled around the keys, she dragged them from beneath the car with Mark still clutching her hand. Pushing herself up, she banged her forehead against the car's side mirror. A burst of pain exploded in her head.

"Ouch!"

"Oh, I'm sorry," he said hastily. "That was my fault." His hand, which had only seconds before enfolded hers, now searched for the tender spot on her forehead. But in his efforts to seek out the injury, his fingers instead brushed against her lips and then his mouth lowered to hers.

"Are you praying?" a familiar voice called.

Hanna clenched her eyes shut in disbelief. How had the moment escaped them? The throb in her head intensified.

"No, Preston," Mark said calmly, teetering back on his knees. "Hanna dropped her keys and bumped her head on the side mirror."

"But I just found them," she said lightly. With Mark's help, she struggled to her feet.

"What about your head?" Mark asked.

"It's all right." She rubbed the spot.

He placed his hands on her upper arms and peered down at her. She heard the anxious tone in his voice. "Do we need to go back inside and get some ice?"

"No. . .no, it will be fine." Hanna hated being the center of attention.

"Are you sure, Miss Stewart?" Preston stepped closer behind Mark.

Hanna pictured the whole youth group gawking at her, at

them, making a big deal over nothing. "Yes, I'm really okay, but thanks for asking." She opened her car door and slid inside.

Mark shook his head. "I'm not so sure you should drive."

She couldn't help but smile at his sweetness, although frustration at the whole parking lot episode pricked her nerves. "I'm absolutely fine."

He closed the door, then leaned down to look at her through the open window. "Will you promise to call me as soon as you get home?" he softly asked.

"I guess," she replied, finding it nearly impossible to tear herself away from his dark eyes. She waved at Preston and the rest of the students, then drove from the restaurant toward home. Suddenly the humiliation of dropping her keys faded with the glory of another realization: Mark had come incredibly close to kissing her!

Her headache was worth it. *I'd have bruised both knees and blackened my eyes for a kiss.* If only Preston hadn't interrupted them. . . .

ten

Hanna entered her apartment humming the last song she'd heard on the car radio. Flipping on the lights, she took a passing glance in the hallway mirror, and the sight of her injured forehead startled her.

"Ooh, looks nasty." She peered closer to scrutinize the swollen, purplish blue lump. Further examination revealed a horizontal indentation matching the corner of the car mirror. *No wonder it hurts,* she thought. Her injury gave a whole new meaning to "goose egg."

She fluffed and arranged her bangs over it and breathed a sigh of relief when her hair successfully covered the unsightly mark. Maybe with a little more makeup no one would notice.

As the pounding pain increased, Hanna headed for the kitchen to fill an ice bag. *I need to call Mark,* she reminded herself, as one more time she relived their evening together. Her heart flipped with the memory of his fingers touching her lips and what could have been next, if not for Preston's untimely interruption.

Hanna sighed happily as she sealed the plastic bag of ice. Mark wore the same cologne he used in high school, and it still had the same intoxicating effect, especially when he was dangerously close.

Headache or not, I'm still tingling to the end of my toes.

The phone rang, halting her reverie. Holding the ice over the lump with one hand, she clumsily grabbed the phone with the other—and dropped it. Thoroughly frustrated, she snatched it up and finally managed a faint "hello."

"Are you still dropping things?" Mark asked, concern mingled with his teasing.

Hanna smiled at his familiar voice and leaned back against the kitchen wall, still clutching the ice to her forehead. "I guess so. At least I didn't hurt myself this time."

"You were supposed to call me," he said accusingly.

"I was fixin' to—just as the phone rang."

"A likely story," he teased. "But, frankly, I shouldn't have let you drive home alone."

"Mark, this is only a bump on the head, for pity's sake. Anyway, I couldn't let you bring me home. We're seen too much together. Remember you have to live above reproach—just as I do. All you or I need is for someone to say something ugly about seeing you here late at night."

"I'm sure I could have gotten the students to chaperon."

She giggled. "You're probably right, but I made it just fine."

"Good. Now have you put ice on your bump?"

"Yes, sir. I'm holding it to my head as we speak." She dabbed the ice bag against her forehead. It felt much too cold and added a different kind of ache.

"Are you sure we don't need to visit the emergency room?"

Hanna laughed. "Quite certain, thank you very much. I have a very hard head, and besides, it doesn't hurt much anymore." She realized the throb had reduced to a minor irritation, or perhaps his soothing voice had chased away the pain. "I promise to take all necessary precautions."

"What about me calling you every two hours to make sure you're coherent?"

"And when do you plan on sleeping?"

"When I'm not checking on you."

"We'll both be zombies tomorrow."

"I think it's a good idea; head injuries are nothing to fool with." He paused for a moment. "You know, Hanna, if it hadn't been for Preston, I would have kissed you tonight."

Her heart skipped a beat at the intimacy of his tone. Maybe it was her nerves kicking in, but suddenly the whole incident in the parking lot seemed incredibly funny. Hanna bit her lip to keep from giggling. "That did cross my mind."

"Well, murder crossed mine. 'Are you praying?' " He mimicked Preston's voice.

They both laughed, and she dropped the ice pack.

"Did I hear a crash?"

"The ice fell."

"Oh," he groaned. "Why am I not surprised? Guess I'd better let you go. Let's see, it's nine-thirty. So I'll call you at eleven-thirty."

"You really are serious. It's not necessary, honestly. I know all the guidelines for a head injury. Besides, it's swollen, which is a good sign."

"Humor me, Miss Stewart. I want to be your personal doctor tonight, and I'm prescribing a couple of aspirin with a wake-up call in two hours. Now, sweet dreams and good night."

She replaced the receiver and gathered up the remains of the broken ice pack. As she stood, her head began to throb again, and she immediately sat down on the floor. Despite the steady ache, she felt incredibly wonderful that Mark cared about her little accident, enough to even interrupt his sleep. . . What a heavenly way to wake up. A slow smile spread across her lips. He had seemed as disappointed by Preston's sudden appearance as she was. *I should have offered a rain check.* She grinned.

Padding off to bed, Hanna knew exactly where her dreams would take her tonight.

❧

At five-thirty, the alarm jolted Mark from a deep sleep. For a moment he couldn't remember why he had set the clock for so early, but as he palmed the shrill bell, he remembered his commitment to call Hanna. True to his word, he had phoned her every two hours throughout the night, making certain she recognized his voice and sounded fully awake. Each time

Hanna insisted her head didn't hurt and she felt fine.

"No nausea or dizziness?" he had asked.

"Not in the least. Mark, why don't you get some rest?"

"I am," he had assured her. "I'll talk to you again in a couple of hours."

Mark smiled in the darkness. He felt responsible for her injury, but he liked having an excuse for those calls. Even more, he liked hearing her sleep-laced voice. . . He could envision her sleepy violet eyes and the curly, caramel-colored hair tousled around her face.

He liked a whole lot of things about Hanna Stewart, not just her beauty. He liked the way she gave her heart to everything she set out to do. Her devotion to the Lord inspired him to keep trudging along, even when the days proved difficult. Lately his feelings for her seemed to mount each time he saw her—strange, but wonderfully true. And tonight, well, he really wanted that kiss. Her lips had to be as soft and sweet as they looked.

After his call, he set the alarm for seven-thirty; an hour later than usual, but he needed a little more sleep. But his mind refused to stop whirling. Even the sound of her voice drove him crazy.

ঌ

Four days later Marie and Hanna browsed through the sale racks at a local boutique.

"So, do you prefer Mark or Ryan?" Marie asked, examining one clothing item after another.

Hanna smiled at her friend's usual directness. She had shared everything about the bump on her head, except the part where Mark tried to kiss her. She hesitated revealing that precious moment, as though telling anyone might spoil the magic. To Hanna, her and Mark's working relationship seemed a bit awkward, or maybe it was her own inability to shut the door on her emotions when she needed to handle church business. Mark appeared perfectly at ease, but then he always had handled himself confidently.

"Well. . .I feel more comfortable with Ryan than Mark," she began.

"I imagine so," Marie said knowingly. "You're still in love with Mark."

Hanna's eyes grew wide. "How do you know?"

"Am I not right?" the older woman asked with a shake of her silver head. Placing a hand on her hip and waving an accusing finger, she grinned. "You tell me you're not head-over-heels in love with Mark Alexander." When Hanna did not respond, Marie whispered triumphantly, "See, I am right."

Hanna ignored her remark and lifted a pale blue blouse from the rack. "Do you like this?"

"Eluding the truth doesn't make it disappear," Marie replied gently. "And yes, I like the color."

Hanna returned the blouse and faced her friend. Shopping didn't seem to interest her today. She had too many other things on her mind. . .and her heart. "Guess I'm confused about my feelings and what to do about them."

"Because of the past?"

"Yes," she frowned. "I don't want to get hurt again, Marie. And no matter how many times I give it over to God, the doubts and insecurities crop up again."

Marie gave her a sympathetic look. "Are you insecure with yourself or the relationship with Mark?"

"I'm secure as a loved child of God, which means I *should* feel more confident around Mark, but I don't." Hanna shrugged her shoulders. "See what an utter basket case I am? I completely relax with Ryan. Why can't I do that with Mark?"

The older woman eyed her thoughtfully. "You have more to lose with him. Let me put it this way. If Ryan suddenly showed up at the jogging trail one morning with another girl, how would you feel?"

Hanna didn't need to ponder the question. "Probably relieved."

"Exactly. Admit it, girlfriend, the lovebug has bitten you. When I first met my husband, I felt self-conscious about everything. I said the wrong things, wore the wrong clothes, felt afraid he might know my thoughts."

"Dropped things?"

"Yeah, that, too."

"So how did you get over it?"

"When he told me he loved me. Something about those words, like an answer to prayer, put my frenzied emotions in proper prospective."

An old, despairing thought raced through Hanna's mind, and she couldn't dispel it. "But what if he never loves me? Am I going to feel like this forever?"

Marie smiled and patted Hanna's arm. "If you believe your love for Mark is from God, and if you truly give this to Him, then He will see you through. You've trusted Him with your eternal home, now trust Him with your love for Mark."

Hanna nodded. She well understood the wisdom of her friend. God had always been there for her, and if He did not want her involved with Mark, then He'd help her overcome the rejection. *But, God, I don't think I could go through that pain again,* she agonized. Memories of the last cotillion floated vividly across the viewing screen of her heart. *Too many years ago to judge the present,* she inwardly told herself.

Suddenly, a still, quiet voice whispered, *You aren't alone, My child. You will never be alone. Take My hand and let Me carry you through. I will never leave you or forsake you.*

eleven

Mark settled back into an overstuffed chair in Pastor Jacobs' office as he waited for the senior pastor to return from a meeting. Glancing around the room appreciatively, he noted how the decor instantly put him at ease. Muted colors of turquoise, gold, and deep maroon looked masculine and yet soothing. The pastor enjoyed horses, and the wallpaper border depicted English gentlemen suited in riding habits, mounted on their steeds. On the wall behind the huge mahogany desk hung the wooded landscape of a well-known artist Mark recognized. Two other paintings held the same calming effect, plus a dimly lit lamp provided a non-threatening atmosphere for counseling.

Wouldn't work with the students, he thought, slightly amused. *They seem to need bright lights, vivid colors, and tons of posters. If the decorating was left up to them, they'd have speakers in every corner and music blaring in surround sound.*

Hearing Pastor Jacobs' voice, he got to his feet.

"Sorry to keep you waiting," the pastor apologized. Closing the glass door behind him, he shook Mark's hand before sitting at his desk.

Instantly, Mark detected a somberness in the determined set of Pastor Jacobs' jaw and the way his eyelids drooped.

"Mark, I appreciate you carving time from your afternoon for me, especially on such short notice." He paused. "I've got a rather serious matter to discuss with you. I spoke to David Bennett this morning."

Mark immediately feared the worst. "Is Josie all right?"

"I have no idea," the pastor replied simply. "When you and

I talked yesterday, I thought perhaps you had misinterpreted David regarding his daughter, but since then I've changed my mind."

"What happened?" Mark frowned, all the while wondering if he had said or done something to upset the Bennetts. Sometimes in his enthusiasm to minister to others he inadvertently offended them.

"Well, let me begin by saying I've known him for over ten years. The man's a deacon, a valued friend, our families have taken vacations together—why, he and I often play golf. So I didn't hesitate to ask about your conversation." Pastor Jacobs sighed deeply before continuing. "David proceeded to tell me that his family's needs came before anything else, which set off an obvious warning signal in my mind. I wondered where God fit in his scheme of things. Anyway, he went on to say his request that Josie not have visitors resulted from a session with their family's psychiatrist."

Mark nodded. "That's pretty much what he told me, too."

"It seems their psychiatrist believes Josie should not have any outside influence except her parents and the new therapist. It's supposed to be conducive to her mental health care."

Mark swallowed his frustration. "I don't understand the reasoning, but then again, I'm not a doctor."

"Frankly, I don't either, and David evaded every question. In fact, he thanked me for calling, but asked that I respect his privacy and tend to church affairs."

"You're kidding!"

"No, I wish I was. He soon ended the conversation due to a business appointment."

Mark chewed on his lower lip, then felt compelled to voice a deep-rooted suspicion. "Do you think Josie is still in the Bennett home?"

Pastor Jacobs eyed him curiously. "You know, I honestly have no idea. It never occurred to me she'd be anywhere else."

"Wouldn't it make sense to you?"

The pastor nodded slowly. "Yes, but where could she be? In a mental hospital?"

"Maybe. A lot of possibilities have crossed my mind—a drug rehab, a home for unwed mothers, or simply someplace other than home."

The silence was deafening, and again Mark waited.

"Sounds like you have been privy to other information." Pastor Jacobs' gray eyes searched Mark's face.

"I may have, I'm not quite sure," he said slowly. He went on to explain the conversation he'd overheard in the hospital. "I guess I could be overreacting," he finished.

"I hope you are," Pastor Jacobs said wearily. "But David's response this morning leads me to believe otherwise. What I've told you is strictly confidential. He could very well call back and have an entirely different outlook. But for right now, all I can do is pray for the family. I certainly don't have any answers."

"Neither do I," Mark replied. "I believe the whole family is in crisis, not just Josie. What else would cause a family to isolate themselves from friends, their pastor, and God?"

The pastor leaned back in his chair. "This morning I had my feathers ruffled, now I'm wondering what God would have us do to help. David is overwhelmed by something, and at this point, he is shutting us all out."

"Pastor, I'll be praying for a softening of his heart," Mark replied. "Right now, no matter what the problem is, he needs his Christian brothers."

❧

Over a week later, on a Saturday morning, Hanna arrived at church to practice a song before Sunday's worship services. She'd been asked to sing as a part of the church's twentieth anniversary celebration, and she wanted to do her best. Afterward, everyone would gather at the church's family-life center for a picnic, games, volleyball, and fellowship. The youth choir was scheduled to perform their musical, and

Hanna was excited about the students' participation. But she would feel much better about her own song after rehearsing.

Part of her own misgivings about singing centered around her preoccupation with Mark. Granted, she did feel a little more relaxed around him lately, and what was even more exciting, he appeared genuinely interested in her! But now she pondered what to do next. *Patience,* she often told herself, but like a child she wanted everything right now. Whatever happened to that independent life she had led before Mark walked back into it? Everything had been smooth and simple. . .teaching at the high school, directing the youth choir, spending time with her parents and friends.

Lately, she had even toyed with telling him about her growing feelings for him.

Releasing a deep breath, Hanna's thoughts turned to Josie; she hoped her family planned to attend the day's events. She had seen them together in church once, but they sat in the balcony and left before she had an opportunity to greet them. Hanna prayed the new counselor had made progress. Ryan had shared his concern for the Bennetts with her, but nothing more. She knew he had spent many hours conferencing with the new therapist about them, but of course Ryan couldn't reveal the confidential information they shared.

Hanna unlocked the front door of the church. Glancing at her watch, she mentally allowed herself an hour and a half to practice before meeting her parents for lunch.

She snapped on a light in the sanctuary and gazed up and around the large auditorium, visualizing it full for both Sunday services. Her eyes rested on the choir loft, and she pictured the many members clothed in creamy robes, beaming as they lifted their voices in praise. The words and notes would not be as important as the emotion on their faces.

God, I pray for lives to be changed tomorrow. I thank You for all the many good people who have helped to make this

*service a real blessing. Be with Pastor Jacobs as he delivers
the message, and I pray for young and old to be touched with
the words You give him. Use me in song to minister to others
as a reflection of Your love and grace.*

Hanna climbed the steps leading to the stage area behind
the pulpit where the grand piano stood. She adjusted the
piano bench and opened the sheet music. The moment her
fingers touched the keys and she began to warm up, she felt a
deep, inner peace.

With a smile, Hanna played the introduction to "Joyful,
Joyful, We Adore Thee," one of her favorite hymns and a
special request from Pastor Jacobs. She'd found an arrangement to the Beethoven piece that combined the original and a
more contemporary version that utilized the entire orchestra.

As Hanna closed her eyes to sing, the melody rang throughout the sanctuary.

"Joyful, joyful, we adore Thee, God of glory, Lord of
     love;
Hearts unfold like flowers before Thee, opening to the
     sun above.
Melt the clouds of sin and sadness, drive the dark of
     doubt away;
Giver of immortal gladness, fill us with the light of day!

"All Thy works with joy surround Thee, earth and
     heaven reflect Thy rays,
Stars and angels sing around Thee, center of unbroken
     praise;
Field and forest, vale and mountain, flowery meadow,
     flashing sea,
Chanting bird and flowing fountain call us to rejoice in
     Thee.

"Thou art giving and forgiving, ever blessing, ever blest,

Wellspring of the joy of living, ocean depth of happy
    rest!
Thou our Father, Christ our Brother—all who live in
    love are Thine;
Teach us how to love each other, lift us to the joy divine.

"Mortals, join the mighty chorus which the morning
    stars began;
Father-love is reigning o'er us, brother-love binds man
    to man.
Ever singing, march we onward, victors in the midst of
    strife;
Joyful music leads us sunward in the triumph song of life."

Twice more she sang all four verses until the sound satis-
fied her. As Hanna began the song yet again, she sensed a
stirring of her spirit to worship God in complete abandon-
ment. Leaving the piano bench, she faced a huge wooden
cross behind the choir loft and lifted her voice in praise.

When Hanna finished, tears rolled down her cheeks. How
she loved the Lord God Almighty. And how He had blessed
her. *Thank You, God, for this special time with You.* She knew
her song stood ready for Sunday because He had prepared
her heart.

❦

Mark blinked the moistness from his eyes as he listened to
Hanna finish her song. He had been at the back of the church
when he first heard the piano and then recognized her deep
alto voice. Planning to surprise her, he had moved toward a
rear entrance with every intention of making himself known.
But what he saw and heard stopped any thought of invading
her private worship. Never had he witnessed such an intimate
moment between God and one of His children. Hanna's
voice rose throughout the sanctuary. Her face radiated the
light of communion with the Creator.

Deep in his spirit, Mark realized what God had been trying to tell him all along: *This was the woman meant for him.* But how did he proceed? Did she feel the same about him?

☙

"I'm so glad you two came," Hanna said happily, as she hugged her parents after the second worship service on Sunday morning. "I know both of you have responsibilities at your church, and this means a lot to me."

"Thank you, sweetheart," her mother said. "When you described the anniversary celebration and announced that you were going to sing, well, we just had to come. The service was simply beautiful—and how thoughtful of your pastor to ask everyone to dress casual."

"Good message, too," her father added. "And you sang like an angel as always."

Hanna wrinkled her nose at him. "You would say that even if I didn't hit a single note right."

He smiled broadly and put his arm around her shoulder. "Remember, I'm your number-one fan."

"*We* are your number-one fans," her mother corrected.

Hanna loved her handsome, silver-headed dad, and her blond, willowy mother. They had always supported her, even when she didn't deserve it.

She glanced up at the crowd and saw Mark approaching them. Instantly, she remembered he hadn't spoken to her father since high school.

"Good morning, Mark," her father greeted, and reached to shake his hand.

Mark smiled and grasped the older man's hand. "It's good to see you again, sir." Turning to Hanna's mother, he said, "It's been a long time, Mrs. Stewart. How are you?"

Hanna watched and listened to her mother respond graciously. She felt warm and tingly standing by the three most treasured people in her life. Her heart sang with the joy of forgiveness and love.

"Are you folks heading for the picnic?" Mark asked.

"We sure are," her father replied. "I'm starved, and I'm looking forward to hearing the youth choir."

"It will be great—look who they have for a director." Mark grinned and gave Hanna a wink.

"Absolutely," her mother agreed. "Mark, would you like to join us?"

Looking surprised but definitely pleased, he turned to Hanna. "Do you mind?"

She laughed. "Of course not. It will be fun."

After a warm walk to the family-life center, the four enjoyed barbecued beef and chicken, potato salad, huge soft rolls, baked beans, buttery ears of corn, and mounds of desserts. Once they had eaten, Mark and Hanna, with the help of several parents, challenged the youth to a game of volleyball—and won. Her mother offered to assist in the face painting, and her father umpired a softball game.

As the afternoon finally drew to a close, the youth assembled to perform their musical. Hanna felt nervous, especially since her parents and Mark were present, but she was confident in the choir's abilities. Within minutes, the student orchestra had set up and tuned their instruments, and the singers were anxious to get started.

Stepping up to the podium, Hanna faced the people of Abundant Grace Church. "Thank you all for being here this afternoon. We are very proud of our youth choir and orchestra, and I'm sure you will enjoy their performance. But before I begin, I want to thank the many wonderful parents and workers who have helped make this musical possible." She smiled from her heart. "I'm sure these students will bless you as they have blessed me. And now I'd like to present to you Abundant Grace's youth choir as they present drama and song." She turned to the students and lifted her hands, signaling their attention. She mouthed the words, "Relax, enjoy yourself. . . Smile. . . Sing to the Lord—and I love you." Then she cued the orchestra and the music began.

When the group finished, the church members stood and applauded. Hanna felt elated, tearfully happy. Pride for the choir seemed to swell inside her. They had done a splendid job, much better than in any rehearsal. She knew God had perfected their every song.

When she stepped down from the podium and hugged the students crowding around her, she remembered Josie. Suddenly Hanna felt immensely selfish. The entire day had been perfect for her in every way, but the Bennett family hadn't been at church or the festivities. Her happiness was suddenly marred with guilt, and her eyes stole to the empty spot where Josie had played flute. She wondered if the teen would ever return to them.

Mark caught her eye and smiled sadly. He obviously sensed her thoughts about Josie, and his expression of empathy warmed her spirit. *How blessed I am,* she told herself, as her eyes swept over the crowd of pleased onlookers. *Lord, don't ever let me forget the joy of this precious moment. Thank You for allowing me to serve You.*

twelve

"Why is it so quiet in here?" Marie asked Hanna as the two walked down the church hallway. Her friend had called earlier suggesting they have lunch before the summer sped by and school enveloped them both.

"The youth left for camp Sunday afternoon and won't be back until late Friday night," Hanna replied, fishing through her shoulder bag for her car keys. "Some of the staff went, too."

"I'm surprised you're not with them," the older woman commented curiously. "Did you just need a break before the mission trip?"

"I thought I did," Hanna replied candidly. "Mark needed someone to coordinate activities for those kids who weren't able to attend camp. Besides, our church teamed up with another one to bring in a guest music minister, so I didn't see a real purpose in my going."

"They didn't need any additional counselors?" Marie questioned.

"No." Hanna shook her head. "Parents really stepped forward this year to help out. Several even took vacation time from their jobs." Retrieving her keys, Hanna pushed open the door leading to the parking lot. A gust of suffocating air took their breath away.

"Whew!" the older woman exclaimed with a shake of her silver head. "With this heat, I bet you're glad to be inside an air-conditioned office."

Hanna gave her a warm smile. "Think I'd rather be with the kids. I miss them more than I thought."

"And Mark?"

A smile played on Hanna's lips. "Oh, maybe, well, all right. Yes, Marie, I miss him, too."

A grin spread across her friend's face and her gray eyes sparkled mischievously. "Has he called?"

Hanna deliberately hesitated before she answered. She knew only too well how Marie's mind flourished with matchmaking thoughts. "No, there aren't any phones there, except for emergency use."

"I'd call this an emergency of the heart."

Hanna rolled her eyes good-naturedly.

"On the bright side, Friday will be here before you know it," her friend continued.

"He leaves on Saturday for a week-long conference in Orlando." Hanna sighed, then instantly regretted allowing her emotions to surface.

Marie smiled. "It just does my heart good to hear of young love."

Hanna giggled as they both slid into the hot car and snapped their seat belts in place. Sticking her key into the ignition, she sobered. "Seriously, Marie, I have no idea how he feels about me, or if he has any thoughts about us at all."

"Take it from a seasoned citizen, I believe he's as hopelessly in love as you are. I can see it in his eyes."

"And *you*," Hanna laughed, adjusting the air conditioning, "are a hopeless romantic. But that's okay. I love you anyway."

Marie lifted her chin, accentuating her rather pointed nose. "You go ahead and laugh; I'm planning a bridal shower."

"Hmm, right now I'm considering lunch. Tea Room okay?"

The older woman nodded. "Perfect—and I think they have bridal showers there, too."

Hanna wrinkled her nose playfully at her friend. She hoped Mark missed her as much as she did him. They were growing closer, at least from her point of view. After working together all day, they often went to dinner or talked on the phone most of the evening. And last week she overheard one of the other pastors teasing him about her.

"Why is it that I always see Hanna in your eyes?" the man had asked with a hearty chuckle. "Or are those stars I see?"

Mark didn't reply.

❧

Mark stepped inside the cool, comfortable cabin he shared with the youth minister who used the same camp facilities. The two men had gotten little sleep since Sunday evening when they arrived. From the regularly scheduled youth events to prayer vigils late into the night, already he felt exhausted. *I must be getting old,* he surmised with a grimace. *I need a nap.*

Reflecting on the two full days of camp, Mark decided the plan to team up both churches' youth groups was an excellent one. They had about the same number of students, and some of them attended the same junior high and high schools. He thought the combination gave all the kids an opportunity to see God work on a larger scale. In his opinion, students tended to isolate themselves in their home church and failed to realize that God moved in every gathering where truth reigned. The mingling of the two groups produced new friendships and challenged them to a stronger walk once they returned to school campuses in the fall.

Mark smiled, remembering the second night of camp. Over thirty students from both churches had committed their lives to Christ. What a praise report! If only Hanna had been there to experience the heartfelt testimonies of the young people. Mark knew it would be nearly impossible to communicate the emotions and power of their worship and social activities. Regretfully, he wished he had included her in the week's program. His secretary could have filled in at the church office. After all, Hanna had been one of the primary leaders of the students before he came as youth minister, and she loved them all as he did.

Instantly, Mark's gaze ventured to the phone resting on a

small knotty pine dresser. His roommate called his wife every night.

Mark felt like he needed to talk to Hanna, just to hear her sweet voice. Besides, he knew she would want to know how God had already answered prayers among the kids. Glancing at the time, he pictured Hanna sitting behind her desk at the church office with a favorite music motif mug filled with vanilla nut decaf coffee, engulfed in so many plants she could barely find workspace.

Sighing deeply, he decided to call her at home later; someone might interrupt, and he wanted her undivided attention. Selfish as it sounded, he understood his feelings. Maybe tonight he could muster enough courage to discuss their relationship. . .and, more important, find out how she felt about him.

◣

Hanna couldn't concentrate on anything. After leaving the office at the end of the day, she had sorted through her mail, washed a load of towels, double-checked to make sure she didn't have a school workshop during the week of the mission trip, and then sat at the piano without a clue as to what to play. *What is wrong with me?* she mentally berated herself. She considered calling a few girlfriends to take in a movie, but socializing with girls didn't interest her either. Searching through her stack of unread books, she considered a Christian romance, but reading about someone else finding love didn't have much appeal.

Plain and simple, she missed Mark, from his dimpled smile to his attempt at jokes. *I'm lonesome for him,* she concluded, feeling both surprised and frustrated with her own emotions. *Like a love-struck teenager, I'm moping around here with a case of the blues.*

Admitting her dilemma and feeling foolish about it, Hanna resolved to find something constructive to do. She snatched up Beethoven's Ninth Piano Sonata, the piece that had secured her a full college scholarship, and dug into the music.

Within an hour, she'd switched from Beethoven to singing and playing hymns and choruses, which helped her melancholy mood. In the middle of "Amazing Grace" the phone rang.

"Hello," she answered lightly.

"Hey," Mark said softly. "I bet you thought you were rid of me for a whole week."

Hanna smiled and a pleasant, warm sensation nibbled at her toes and rose to the ends of her curly hair. "You mean I'm not?"

"No, I couldn't let you off that easily. Besides, I've heard some great jokes," he said with a lift in his voice.

Hanna moaned. "I knew I should have gone to a movie."

He chuckled and they both shared a laugh. "I'm definitely hurt now," Mark insisted. "Guess I'll get over it. Seriously, the week has been great."

"I'm so glad. How are the kids?"

"Wonderful. Remember how I wondered if sharing camp with another church might be a problem? Well, it's been a real blessing. Some of the kids have made decisions for Christ, and others have rededicated their lives."

Hanna felt her eyes moisten. "Can you tell me which ones?"

"Sure. Ah, let's see. . . Ashla brought her two friends to camp, and both of them came forward. So did Rory, Jason, Alex, and three junior high boys whom I'd never met until camp. Lisa brought four girls and all of them surrendered their lives to Jesus. One of them has a powerful testimony about drugs and alcohol. Oh, you won't believe this one: Daniel went forward, too."

"Daniel!" she squealed. "We've been praying for him since last year's camp."

"Oh, Hanna, he cried like a baby. And so did I. We called his dad, and he whooped and hollered. In fact, he came up for last night's services."

She smiled into the phone. "I wish I could have been there."

"Me, too. I've kicked myself a hundred times for not insisting that you join us."

Hanna tilted her head and kept right on smiling. "And what would I have done? You needed someone to hold down the home fort."

"I'd rather have you here with me, fighting the Indians. I really miss you."

"You're sweet." Hanna heard her doorbell. "Can you hold on a minute, Mark? Someone is at the door."

"Sure, just don't forget about me."

When she answered the door, she was surprised to find Ryan. Smartly dressed in khaki slacks and a name brand knit shirt, as usual he looked as though he had just walked off the cover of a magazine. He carried a bouquet of roses and wore an equally charming smile.

"Ryan, how nice to see you," she said.

He presented her with the roses, and she couldn't resist burying her nose in a fragrant flower. "You sounded so sad this morning with the students gone at camp that I thought I'd try to brighten your evening."

"How thoughtful, and these are lovely. Thank you so much. Would you like to come in?"

Ryan stepped inside. "I hoped you'd ask. I also wondered if I could interest you in dinner and possibly a movie."

She tilted her head. "I'd planned to spend a quiet evening at home."

"Nonsense," Ryan said with a wave of his hand. "Let me take you out, put some laughter into your sweet, lovely face."

When she looked reluctant, he gave his best pleading look. "Please. I promise to have you back early."

Hanna shook her head at him. *Why couldn't he have been Mark?* Perfect flowers, perfect invitation, but wrong man. "Just a minute, Ryan. I have someone on the phone. Won't you have a seat?"

He grinned at her, then walked into the living room and sat on an antique blue and gold Victorian sofa. He looked very much out of place, and the sight forced a laugh from her.

Hanna returned to Mark. "Hi, I'm sorry to keep you waiting." She wished Ryan hadn't chosen such an inopportune time to visit.

"Well, I heard your visitor." Mark's voice had an edge. "So I'll let you go to dinner."

"But I. . ." Hanna began, regret scratching at her nerves.

"Gotta run," he interrupted. "Evening services start in five minutes. Didn't mean to disturb you. 'Bye."

She felt a knot in her stomach as she replaced the phone. She didn't care one bit for his brisk good-bye. So what if Ryan stopped by? He and she were simply friends, running buddies. Why should Mark care? Didn't they have a working relationship?

For a moment Hanna thought Mark might be jealous. But she quickly tossed the thought aside. But he had said he missed her. Glancing at Ryan, the thought crossed her mind that if she was the type to play games, she would accept Ryan's invitation. He certainly had indicated his interest enough times. Yet going out with him because Mark might be envious didn't sound like a godly venture. In fact, the moment the thought crept into her mind, she detested the implication.

Walking into the living room, she faced Ryan. "I'm sorry, but I really don't feel like dinner tonight." She avoided his disappointed look. "I appreciate your thoughtfulness, and the roses are gorgeous, but I'd rather stay home."

≈

Dinner! Roses!

Mark punched his fist into his palm. *Stupid, stupid, stupid,* he admonished himself. *Lord, I really blew that. Now, I'll be lucky if she ever speaks to me again, especially since it's evident that Henderson knows how to entice a lady when she's most vulnerable.*

Sucking in his breath, he decided to call back later and apologize for his rudeness. *Here I am at church camp teaching students about their relationship with Jesus Christ, and I can't even respond to the woman I love—in love!*

He grasped his Bible and checked his watch. Yes, he had plenty of time. He would make the time to talk to God about his jealousy.

thirteen

Hanna closed her Bible, zipped up the soft ivory leather cover, and laid it on her nightstand. She had been reading and studying the seventh and eighth chapters of Romans, which she called the gateway to eternity, basking in the many wonderful words God had given Paul. He wrote with such transparency, letting the reader see and feel that his struggles with sin were the same as theirs. The chapters flowed with an outpouring of the Holy Spirit to believers, with Him interceding in their behalf before the Father and equipping them to resist the temptation of the evil one. As always, the glory belonged to Jesus. Finally Paul simply asked that if God was for us, who could be against us?

Remembering the students at camp and their new decisions for Christ, Hanna prayed their faith would increase once they reached home. She thought of suggesting to Mark that he have a study of Romans for the kids; it seemed fitting. Too many times she had seen friends and family remind new believers of past sins, but Roman 8:1 said it perfectly: "Therefore, there is now no condemnation for those who are in Christ Jesus." Hanna prayed for the students to find strength, hope, and joy in their relationship with Jesus Christ.

Clicking off the bedside lamp, Hanna sank into her pillow and let her thoughts reflect on other things. Mark's strange behavior still bothered her, or rather upset her. Perhaps something pressing had caused him to shorten their conversation. After all, she had been at camp in his position, and she knew firsthand the concerns and problems of students. Some had pertinent questions and things they desperately needed to discuss—right then. A few kids required ministry

112

twenty-four hours a day, and someone could first hear God's call at any hour of the day or night. Mulling all this over in her mind, Hanna then prayed for all the camp workers who gave of themselves to the students.

I'm sure there's a good explanation, she told herself decisively. *Anything could have happened while I left Mark dangling on the phone.*

In the fogginess bordering between sleep and wakefulness, Hanna heard the phone ring. Slowly, she picked up the receiver and answered it softly, as though the darkness required her to whisper.

"Are you in bed?" Mark asked cautiously.

Instantly, her senses sharpened to the sound of his voice. "I'm in bed, but not asleep," she replied, sitting upright and switching on the lamp. "There, the light's on, and you have my full attention. So what's up?"

Mark sighed. "I owe you an apology for earlier this evening."

She hesitated to answer. Her earlier hurt resurfaced. No matter what the reason, he had been rude.

"Can I explain?" he asked. "Or are you too angry to hear me out?"

"No, I'll listen," she replied. "Go ahead."

"Well, I behaved like a fool tonight, a jealous one at that."

Hanna slowly exhaled. So, she had been right in her first assumption, but his confession made her feel uncomfortable. She would rather believe he stood above that sort of thing. Then her thoughts trailed back to her earlier Bible reading from Romans 7, where Paul acknowledged his desire to do good but the inability to carry it out.

"Hanna, I'm sorry I snapped at you. It's none of my business whom you date or see, and I hope I didn't ruin your evening. I'm embarrassed about the way I acted."

She smiled and envisioned the little flecks of gold in his brown eyes. "You didn't spoil my evening. Although, I did find myself wondering what upset you."

"A case of the green-eyed monster," he said grimly. "Really, Ryan Henderson is a fine man. I don't know what got into me. . . Well, yes, I do. My ego took over and I reacted more like an unbeliever than a Christian. I've asked God's forgiveness, and now I'm asking yours."

"Yes, of course. Don't be concerned about me."

"But I am."

Silence hung between them, and since Hanna didn't know what to say, she waited for him to speak.

"This is probably not the best time, and I should be talking to you in person," Mark began. "But I really need to say something."

"Is there a problem?"

"No, at least I hope not. I wondered if you might consider us. . .you know, in a relationship."

Suddenly Hanna felt her emotions whirling, but she refused to fall prey to her own whimsical dreams and desires.

"We're the greatest of friends," she replied, not ready to voice her true feelings.

"I. . .I don't want to be just friends," he stammered. "I know friendships are important, but I'd like for us to be more than that."

"So what are you suggesting, Mark?"

He sighed again. "You're not going to make this easy for me, are you?" He chuckled nervously. "And none of this sounds like I wanted. Hanna, I really care about you."

She had longed for his endearing words since they were sixteen years old. But now that he had spoken them, she felt strangely wary, as though sharing her emotions might chase him away. Or worse yet, her fragile feelings might be dashed again. Her heart soared while a note of warning rang like a bell. "Have you prayed about it?"

"Yes," he said confidently. "And I'm asking if you'll do the same. I really believe God has put you back into my life for a reason."

Hanna paused to savor his words. "Okay, I'll pray about us. I certainly want to be in God's will."

More of the same heavy silence followed.

"Is there a possibility that you might have the same feelings?" he finally asked.

"Possibly," she said, not willing to commit herself, not really understanding her vagueness.

"Can we talk when I get back?"

"Yes, I think we should. When did you have in mind?" Her voice sounded strained, foreign.

"Well, we get in Friday early evening, and I leave Saturday noon for Orlando. What about Friday night?"

"That would be fine. I'd planned to meet the buses, anyway."

"Good, we can arrange something then—and Hanna?"

"Hmm?"

"Thanks for listening. I really miss you."

She couldn't help but smile. "And I miss you, too. I'll see you on Friday."

She replaced the phone, knowing full well sleep would elude her now. Had she been dreaming? Or had he actually said he cared? And why did she feel a twinge of fear?

Trembling, she turned off the light and attempted to sort out her misgivings. She loved Mark, she had for years, which was probably why no other man had ever interested her. Granted, Ryan had all the characteristics of a godly husband, but being with him left her feeling empty, yearning for a different man.

But Mark had hurt her once, and every time she thought she had gotten past the cotillion ball, the old ache seared her heart again.

Dread inched across her soul as the truth whispered gently. She might have forgiven Mark, but had she forgiven herself for the way she behaved back then? Just the thought of those angry years when bitterness and sarcasm laced every word made her wince. *Heavenly Father, I'm not sure why I suddenly feel so afraid of a relationship with Mark. Help me to forgive myself for all of those bitter years. Lord, I'm so ashamed of the way I acted then. Guide me to Your will and make me more like You.*

ও

Hanna pushed the grocery cart past the bakery section with its enticing aroma of fresh baked bread, strolled leisurely along the glass-encased deli meats and cheeses, and then went on to the fresh produce department. She had a craving for avocados and Portabella mushrooms, and they were on sale, but the tomatoes also caught her eye. The longer she lingered, the more fruits and vegetables piled into her cart. Broccoli crowns in green bouquets, and snow-white cauliflower along with ripe bananas and pineapple set her mouth watering.

Never go to the grocery store hungry, she admonished, but too late, the damage had been done. A quart of skim milk and a carton of cottage cheese later, she remembered a sale on tuna steaks and decided to meander in that direction. There, in the frozen food aisle between the French fries and TV dinners, Hanna spotted Linda Bennett.

She hadn't seen or spoken to the woman since Josie's hospital stay, and Hanna felt apprehensive about approaching her. After all, her husband had made clear that she and Mark were not to contact their daughter. Yet, remembering their last conversation—a pleasant one—she simply couldn't ignore Josie's mother.

Taking a deep breath as she prayed for wisdom, she angled her cart in the other woman's direction.

"Hi, Mrs. Bennett."

The attractive brunette turned and smiled warmly. Her response immediately put Hanna at ease. "Well, hello, Hanna. It's good to see you." Her eyes held no pretense, only sincerity.

"Is everything going well?" Hanna asked a bit hesitantly.

Mrs. Bennett's lips quivered, but she lifted her chin and controlled her emotions. "As well as can be expected," she replied. "Josie is making progress, but it's. . .it's a struggle."

Hanna saw her pain as she blinked back the tears moistening her eyes. She wanted to rush to Mrs. Bennett's side and place a comforting arm around her, but instead she swallowed the lump forming in her own throat and gripped the grocery cart. Times like these, she regretted being so emotional. Her feelings seemed to stop her cold and tie her in knots when she really wanted to reach out in Christian love. Finally she managed to say, "I'm praying for all of you."

"I know you are, and we feel your prayers. Things have been so difficult, and David and I regret the stands we have to make, even to the point of sacrificing friendships." Pausing, she bit her lower lip. "I guess I've said too much." She reached inside her purse and dabbed her eyes. Seconds later, she lifted her head and forced a smile. "Everything will be fine; I have to believe that. God will see us through."

Hanna abandoned her cart and made her way to Mrs. Bennett. Tears clouded her vision as she patted the woman's hand. "If there is anything I can do to help, please call."

"Thank you. Just keep us in your prayers, and I will tell Josie I saw you."

"Good. And tell her I love her, would you?"

Mrs. Bennett nodded through a fresh onslaught of tears, and Hanna reached out to hug her shoulders, despite her own wet eyes.

"When it's all over, we'll sit down and talk," Mrs. Bennett finally said. "Until then, I must abide by my husband's wishes."

"I understand," Hanna replied, and the two women parted.

Driving home from the grocery store, she contemplated every word and gesture during the conversation with Linda Bennett. She had seemed glad to see Hanna, yet she was obviously full of turmoil and pain. What could be so devastating that she and her husband refused the friendship and support of

fourteen

Hanna cringed at Pastor Jacobs' announcement. One of the buses had broken down en route home, and the repairs could delay the passengers up to four hours. If all went well, they would arrive sometime after ten o'clock that night. Unfortunately, it happened to be Mark's bus. Deeply disappointed, she suddenly had an urge to hop into her own little car and go after him. But what about the other passengers? She could hear her feeble explanation now.

"Sorry, everyone, I only drove up here for Mark. You see, we need to have a discussion about our relationship, and if we don't talk tonight then it will have to wait until after his trip to Orlando and the mission trip."

Selfish, aren't you? she inwardly accused. She realized this delay simply added to her apprehension about Mark. *Okay, Lord, You have my attention,* she conceded. *I'll go home and spend time with You.*

After informing the pastor that she'd return at ten to meet the late bus, Hanna drove home. Although she had looked forward to meeting with Mark, she still felt unprepared to talk about their relationship.

I'm a wimp! she angrily accused. *And a coward! There's no reason for this queasiness in the pit of my stomach each time I try to sort out my emotions.* Raising her chin in a stubborn stance, she determined to work through all of her feelings.

Once inside her apartment, she collected her Bible, pen, and paper. Curling up on the sofa, she prayed for guidance to release the heaviness burdening her thoughts. She would do whatever God wanted, even if it meant telling Mark that she didn't have peace about the two of them together. As devastating as that sounded, at least she would feel secure if she knew God's will. And Hanna wanted, above all things, to be obedient to God.

But a half hour ticked by and still an empty sheet of paper glared up at her. Usually writing down her problems helped her weed out the real concerns plaguing her mind. But she couldn't bring herself to lift the pen. Finally, painstakingly she wrote: *I don't know why I feel so uncertain about a relationship with Mark, when I've prayed for this very thing.* Countless explanations rose and fell, but she failed to pinpoint any particular one.

Opening her Bible, the eighth chapter of Romans drew her again. She read it diligently, praying through each verse, looking for what God wanted her to see. At last she reached verse 12:

"Therefore, brothers, we have an obligation—but it is not to the sinful nature, to live according to it. For if you live according to the sinful nature, you will die; but if by the Spirit you put to death the misdeeds of the body, you will live, because those who are led by the Spirit of God are sons of God. For you did not receive a spirit that makes you a slave again to fear."

Hanna felt her heart flutter, and she reread the last sentence aloud: " 'For you did not receive a spirit that makes you a slave again to fear.' " For certain, fear had its clutches wrapped around her like a vise. But what exactly was she afraid of?

Unwanted emotions floated through her mind. What if she got fat again? What if Mark's attraction was based solely on his guilt about the past? What if she was in love with love and not the man? Could she ever make a commitment that meant sharing every facet of her life? Resigned to tears, she finally understood that only the heavenly Father could give her the peace she so desperately needed.

Picking up the sheet of paper, she slowly wrote: *fear of the unknown*. Hanna sighed heavily, realizing she had always been a control person, and very independent. Her music, volunteer work, exercise, diet, daily schedule—even God had a neat little slot. Her life appeared to be in fastidious order. She had thought she relied solely upon the Lord for everything, but now she realized otherwise. All this time she had believed God ruled her life, when really He simply took the space she had assigned to Him.

Oh, God, how wrong I've been. Conviction seared her heart and mind. *I trusted You for eternal life, but not for my life here on earth. No wonder I'm afraid of a relationship with Mark. I couldn't ever give myself unselfishly to him when I can't do the same for You. I love You, Father, and I am so sorry for not giving You complete control. You are the Lord and Master of my life, and from this moment on I give You all of me. Forgive my foolish ways.*

Chewing on her lip, Hanna turned to the words in 1 John 4:18, which said, *"There is no fear in love. But perfect love drives out fear."*

With tears streaming down her face, she slipped from the sofa to her knees. God wanted all of her; she had been adopted as His child and He loved her unconditionally. Hanna saw it now. She had no reason to fear love or the unforeseen future, for the Creator cradled her destiny. No matter what happened with Mark, God would be right there with her every step of the way. He would give her joy and peace, now and forever.

Hanna looked back on her life and Mark's, and saw how God had taken two lost kids, touched their hearts, and nurtured them into spiritual maturity, in order to bless them with His gift of love. How very wrong of her to refuse such a blessing, and how sorry she felt for not trusting Him.

For the first time Hanna felt a peace about Mark. More important, she rested secure in her relationship with God. A statement made in Bible study came to mind: Salvation is a gift from God; holiness is a pursuit. *Lord, guess I'll be in pursuit until I see You face to face,* she realized with a rueful smile. *But why does it have to hurt so much?*

Shortly before ten o'clock, Hanna drove to the church. A group of parents and Pastor Jacobs had gathered around to wait for the late bus. One of the mothers had brought enough sandwiches and sodas to feed the entire youth group. Another baked twelve dozen chocolate chip cookies. The night air proved pleasant, and they all chatted until after twelve when the latecomers finally arrived.

Forty tired and worn passengers stumbled from the creaking vehicle. Tousled hair, smeared mascara around the girls' eyes, and wrinkled clothing characterized the motley group. A few hugged pillows to their chests and some carried their shoes, but all appeared glad to be home.

Hanna watched Mark step down from the bus. He quickly scanned the crowd, but she didn't want to announce her presence like an immature teen. His eyes suddenly captured hers, and a broad smile spread across his face. At the mere sight of him, Hanna felt her stomach flutter, and her heart pounded inside her chest. She lifted her hand and waved, returning his smile.

She waited while he helped the students find their belongings. His calm voice soothed the effects of the long drive home, both with the kids and the impatient parents. In the shadowy darkness, lit only by the streetlights, she saw he looked exhausted, and her heart went out to him for his humble, giving spirit.

A quick glance at all of the kids and parents hovering around the luggage compartment convinced her that Mark needed help. She moved to the open bin below the bus and pulled out a sleeping bag into the light. Reading the identification tag, she called out the owner's name. A girl quickly claimed it, and Hanna dragged out another bag to find its owner. A camp counselor and a parent followed her lead, and soon the weary travelers were on their way home, equipped with the additional bonus of sandwiches, sodas, chocolate chip cookies—and most important, a deeper relationship with God.

"Thanks," Mark said, once the last carload drove away. They were the only two people left in the parking lot now. "You were absolutely incredible." He leaned against the side of the church and jammed his hands into his pockets. She felt his gaze slowly meander over her features.

"You're welcome," she replied, nearly bursting with love.

An understanding smile passed between them. She realized that in a few short hours he would need to pack his things for the Orlando trip. He was already working on a sleep deficit, and the coming week promised to be just as grueling. "Mark, you really need some rest. Why don't you let me take your dirty clothes, wash them up, and have them up here by eleven in the morning?"

He grimaced. "Not on your life. Sweaty socks, mud-caked shorts, and a food-fight T-shirt. Whew, what a mess. And the smell is downright embarrassing. I wouldn't ask my own mother to do that."

She flashed him a grin. "That's why I'm volunteering."

"No, Hanna. I won't let you do my laundry." He shook his head and reached down for his suitcase.

"Are you afraid I'm going to run off with your stuff?" she teased.

"Maybe." He chuckled. "Can't be too careful in the big city. Truthfully, I can handle it, but you are so sweet to offer. I had hoped we could find time to talk."

"As tired as you are?" She picked up his duffel bag. "I'm not going anywhere, and you need your rest."

"Really?" He reached to take the bag from her. His hand gently clasped over the top of hers, and her pulse quickened as she remembered a similar incident in another parking lot.

"Yes, really," she replied shyly. Her eyes slowly trailed up his hands, arms, broad shoulders, face, and finally reached his eyes. Although the darkness hid their color and depth, she felt their gaze probing hers. For a timeless moment neither of them spoke.

"I had my doubts," he said, his hand still clamped over hers. "You didn't sound very enthusiastic the other night."

"Um, I had a little soul-searching to do."

"Did you find what you were looking for?"

"Absolutely." Hanna felt electrical impulses from the bottom of her stomach to the tips of her fingers. She trembled.

"You're shaking," Mark said softly. "Can't be from this heat."

Slowly, he lowered the duffel bag. As she released her hold on it, he entwined his fingers with hers. He stepped closer, and with his other hand, cupped her chin and tilted it slightly. "Preston's not around, is he?" he whispered.

"No," she murmured, "haven't seen him."

"Wonderful," he breathed. Time suspended around them as his lips descended on hers, gently brushing. . .tenderly teasing. . .silently asking permission to deepen his kiss.

Without a moment's hesitation, she slipped her arm around his neck and buried her fingers in his thick, dark hair. His hand slid to her waist and inched across her back, drawing her closer. As she had always imagined, his embrace felt strong and firm. When his lips pressed more firmly against hers, she responded with more fervor than she ever knew existed within her. Sensing the danger of unchecked emotions, she eased back from him.

Reluctantly, they parted and Mark stepped back, still grasping her hand. "I think I can go another week without sleep now."

She laughed lightly, feeling warm, bathed in the moment. "Will that do until we can talk?"

"You bet, but I'm wide awake now."

"Except you need your rest."

"You said that before."

She tugged on his hand. "Come on and walk me to my car. Once I'm gone, you won't have an excuse not to go home."

Still holding onto her, he picked up the duffel bag and the suitcase. "I don't intend to let go of you that easily."

"I see," she giggled. "And you're sure you don't want me to wash your things?"

"Nope. But there is something you *can* do."

She felt herself grinning from the inside out. "Okay," she said in mock annoyance. "What is it?"

"Let me call you every night from Orlando, and. . ." He swung her around to face him. "Let me kiss you one more time, before you leave me alone in this dark parking lot."

"Poor thing," she whispered. "Have to think about it."

But before she could say more, he stole a kiss just as they reached her car.

"We still need to talk," he commented as he opened her door. "But I don't know when. Not over the phone."

She wet her lips and smiled sweetly. "Maybe before school starts."

He groaned. "And break my heart? This is the end of July. You're talking about weeks from now."

"After the mission trip?" She laughed.

"Guess that's the best we can do," he said with a sorrowful smile. "Hey, are you coming up here to see me off tomorrow?"

"I can," she replied, "but aren't you afraid of the talk it might generate?"

He leaned into the car and grinned. "No, ma'am, I think I'd like it."

Hanna had to smile at his answer, because she felt exactly the same way.

fifteen

Mark slammed shut the crowded overhead compartment bin of the airplane and slid into a window seat. After strapping the safety belt securely around him, he adjusted the air conditioner vent to cool his face. Exchanging a smile with him, Pastor Jacobs took the aisle seat beside him. Both men were quiet, and Mark surmised neither of them had gotten much sleep the night before.

A quick glance at his watch revealed only a few minutes until takeoff, and then he would nap or he'd never make it through the hectic pace of the next week. Last night, or rather early this morning, after washing his clothes, he had fallen into bed only to find he couldn't sleep for thinking about Hanna and the miraculous change in her.

After making a complete fool of himself last week at camp, he had wondered whether she would ever speak to him again. She had sounded so indecisive about the two of them discussing a relationship, and he couldn't blame her considering the way he had reacted to Ryan showing up at her apartment. In fact, Mark had believed her feelings swayed toward the guy. After all, how could he compete with roses and dinner? And she saw Ryan every morning! Mark had even entertained taking up jogging rather than working out at the gym, but that would be too obvious. They would look like the three musketeers—or the three stooges.

His dilemma with Hanna had badgered his thoughts all through the last day of camp, and if not for his strong reliance upon the Lord, it would have destroyed his joy with the students.

That morning, Mark's quiet time had reflected on Philippians 4. Such a powerful, rich chapter. How many times had he quoted and preached to the youth about Paul's encouraging letter to the believers in Philippi? He continued to read until verse 12: " 'I know what it is to be in need, and I know what it is to have plenty. I have learned the secret of being content in any and every situation, whether well fed or hungry, whether living in plenty or in want.' " The phrase about contentment seemed to leap off the page.

His mind reflected back over the hard times in college as a new believer and how he had faced insurmountable financial worries and criticism when he felt led to quit football. He remembered his concerns about his sisters and widowed mother. . .the call to ministry and his friends' negative responses. How many times had God proven Himself faithful? He had carried him through one rough journey after another, just as His Word promised.

Now, Mark slowly began to feel the presence of God; He *was* sufficient for whatever lay ahead. Mark loved Hanna, and the Father knew his heart. A sense of peace rested a comforting hand upon his shoulders. The doubt plaguing his mind about her dissipated, and in its place he felt excitement that God was moving.

Mark inwardly smiled at the memory of last night with Hanna. Her sweet spirit and request to wash his clothes astounded him. She had always been giving and generous, but at a distance, as though a wall separated them. Many times he had felt frustrated and wanted to give up, especially after the evenings when they had shared an intimate phone conversation, only to have her avoid him the next morning. What a wonderful, awesome, totally God-like change.

Now, I'm sounding like one of the kids, he thought, thoroughly amused. *But I'm so lucky. . .and she has the softest lips.*

The voice of the stewardess explaining safety procedures

interrupted his thoughts. *Back to what's happening now,* he told himself and tried to listen to the pleasant woman's instructions.

"I hope you're planning to sleep," Pastor Jacobs commented, once she finished speaking.

Mark closed his eyes and nodded. "Yes, sir. I'm not ashamed to admit that I'm not as young as I used to be. I've got more sore muscles than I knew existed. Why do teenage boys think they have to prove their manliness by wrestling?"

The pastor chuckled. "Now you know why I only visit camp for a few days—and when I do, I don't torment my body in wrestling matches or compete in sports that are bound to throw my back out. I learned my lesson a long time ago; I'll let you young fellas keep up with them."

"Well, I'm having my doubts today," Mark replied with a yawn, and they laughed.

"Seriously, you're doing an excellent job." The pastor smoothed back what little hair he had left. "The kids love you, and the parents are really pleased. I see we've added to the youth group, and from the number of decisions made for Christ last week, you are definitely in the middle of God's work."

Mark waved his hands in front of him to protest. "Be careful with the compliments. I'm only picking up the strands of what Hanna started. They had an excellent leader before I came."

Pastor Jacobs gave him a wry grin. "Do I detect something other than admiration for our Hanna?"

Mark felt his face redden. Some of the other pastors had teased him about her, but not the senior pastor. "Possibly. I mean I'd like for there to be."

"Oh, it's quite obvious—for the both of you," the pastor said good-naturedly. "When I was at camp, I saw that moonstruck look in your face. And then back at the office, I caught the same stars in Hanna's eyes."

Mark grimaced. "I wonder who else can tell?"

The pastor chuckled. "Everyone, I'm sure. Folks are whispering all over the church."

Mark shook his head. "No use denying it; she sure is special."

The pastor smiled knowingly. He chuckled and closed his eyes. Mark heard the comment "Young love," but he didn't respond.

The aircraft raced down the runway, and as it increased velocity, the roar of the jet engines thrusting it forward echoed in his ears. It lifted up smoothly, and he watched the objects below grow smaller and smaller. He noticed that the pastor pulled out a stick of gum and smiled. Mark loved flying and he never had a problem with high altitude.

"Can you tell me about the pastors' conference?" he asked a few moments later.

"Sure, let's see. It's always jam-packed with seminars, starting at eight in the morning and going until nearly midnight."

Mark groaned, and the pastor laughed. "Didn't you go last year?"

"No, I was involved with a student camp."

"Well, my advice to you is skip the 'get acquainted' hour before dinner and take an extra nap. You'll need it."

"I may take your advice." Mark pulled a brochure from his day planner that explained the scheduled week of activities. "I see the list of speakers is quite impressive. One of my seminary buddies plans to be there, too."

The pastor nodded. "Then you'll need all the rest you can get."

Mark replaced the brochure and zipped up the planner. Closing his eyes once more, he decided to take the much-needed nap, but an urgent matter refused to leave him alone. *I've got to ask about Josie,* he thought wearily. "By any chance have you heard from the Bennetts?"

The older man leaned back in his seat before answering, and Mark wondered if he had heard the question. Just as he considered asking it again, Pastor Jacobs replied. "As a matter of fact, I intended to talk to you about the Bennetts."

Immediately his senses perked up. "Can we talk now?"

"The young are so impatient," Pastor Jacobs muttered, "but then I was once, too." Chuckling, he went on. "Seriously, David called me the morning I drove up to camp. I'd hoped to discuss the conversation with you then, but we were all busy with the students."

"If you'd rather wait until later. . ."

"Not at all," he declared with a shake of his head. "Frankly, there's little to tell. He apologized for the previous time we spoke and told me things were beginning to improve."

"Good," Mark breathed. "Praise God."

"Surprisingly enough, he mentioned that the three of them were involved in family counseling in a prayerful effort to end Josie's problem."

"Did he give any indication as to what kind of problem she has?"

"No, but he did say I could share his conversation with you and Hanna."

Mark's eyes widened. "Sounds like the family's made progress already."

The pastor gave him a hopeful nod. "Seems to be the case. Anyway, David wants you both to know how much he and Linda value and appreciate your friendship with their daughter. And when this is all over, he'd like to sit down and explain what happened with her and why they felt it necessary to isolate her from everyone."

Immediately Mark felt a mixture of exhilaration and relief. He knew the thrill of answered prayer. "Now, that is great," he responded. "Have you told Hanna?"

"No, I wanted to tell you first, or both of you together, but it didn't work out that way. You can, if you'd like." He grinned. "I certainly wouldn't want you running out of things to talk about."

Mark returned the grin. "Thanks."

"Now, I don't know about you, but I need this flight time to catch up on sleep."

"Um, I agree," Mark replied, and eased back into his seat. Just a few days ago, he had fought depression with a vengeance, but now everything seemed to be falling right into place. . . .

⋅⋅⋅

Mark unpacked his week's worth of clothes into the drawers and closet of the hotel room. His roommate, the minister of education, had gone ahead to the "get acquainted" hour before dinner, but Mark had elected to catch up on his sleep. Refreshed after napping on the plane and then extending it for another hour, his thoughts sped to the week ahead. He had looked forward to the pastors' conference for months, especially the sessions designated for evangelism and working with the youth.

Closing his luggage and setting it aside, he noticed the clock gave him thirty minutes to spare. Grinning, he snatched up the phone and punched in Hanna's number. Hopefully, Ryan Henderson wouldn't arrive to whisk her off to dinner—but if he did, Mark intended to handle it much more diplomatically than before.

The phone rang three times. When the answering machine picked up on the fourth ring, his spirits took a nosedive.

"Hi, Hanna," he began. "This is. . ."

"Hi, Mark," a familiar, feminine voice said, out of breath. "Sorry, I've been running, and I heard the phone as I unlocked the door."

He laughed. "Don't you get enough exercise before breakfast?"

"Um," she replied, "I didn't go this morning. Slept in."

"Late date?" he asked, smiling and envisioning her teardrop eyes.

"Dreadfully late," she replied with a sigh. "And I had a wonderful time."

"I'm so glad," he continued. "Anybody I know?"

"Ah, yes. Was it you?"

"Right! You've just won the jackpot!"

"Really? What did I win?"

"A phone call from Orlando, Florida, from a wonderful guy who has charm, wit, and. . ."

"Humility," she finished, and they both laughed. "Did you have a good flight?"

"Smooth and easy—at least I guess so. I slept."

"So are you all rested and ready for the conference?"

"Yeah. Actually, I'm pretty excited about it, but Pastor Jacobs gave me some bad news."

"Oh, I'm sorry."

Mark lay back on the bed with his feet dangling off the side. "He informed me that the week's schedule begins at eight and ends close to midnight."

"Sounds tough. I hope you aren't planning to call me after putting in a hard day," she said gently.

"Well, I'd like to."

"Mark, your rest is more important. Don't forget, you'll be back only a few days before the mission trip. I'd rather you crawl into bed so you can better handle the conference."

He hesitated. Her concern for him was one more reason why he loved this lady. "You are the most incredible woman I've ever met. I am so blessed." Silence was his only answer, and then he thought he heard muffled sobs. "Hanna, what's wrong. Are you crying?"

"Yes," she finally managed. "That was the sweetest thing to say. Thank you."

He heard the door unlatch and his roommate stepped inside. He looked up to see his old friend from seminary with him. *What timing,* he thought regretfully. *And I wanted to tell her about the Bennetts.* "You are more than welcome, but it's true." He watched his roommate make a huge heart with his hands and blow him a kiss. His friend burst into laughter.

How did they know who he was talking to?

"Who's there?" she asked with a faint sniff.

"Oh, Brad just walked in with an old friend. Remember I told you about him?"

"Yes, the guy from seminary. Well, as much as I'd like to talk, you probably should visit."

"If you don't mind," he replied reluctantly. "Can I call you later?"

"Of course. I'll be right here. Enjoy your evening."

Mark hung up the phone with a bittersweet feeling. He knew the evening would be enjoyable, but he would much rather be talking to the sweet voice on the other end of the phone line.

sixteen

Hanna expelled a long breath as she jogged into the second mile. The first mile always seemed to be the most difficult, no matter how well she stretched out beforehand. Now, she could enjoy the run, even in the rapidly rising humidity.

"Did you say you would be gone for ten days?" Ryan asked, keeping pace with her.

"Actually eleven. We'll leave on Saturday morning and be back on a Tuesday." Her mind danced with the prospect of spending all that time with Mark.

"I'll have no one to jog with." He sounded a bit dejected.

"Oh, you'll probably cover three extra miles each morning," she teased, ignoring his plea for sympathy.

"I don't think so. It won't be the same without you. I've really enjoyed our starting out each new day together."

His tone gave her chill bumps in the morning heat. She definitely heard the passion in his voice, and it unnerved her.

"I think we need to talk," she replied seriously. Although she had suspected Ryan's emotions ran deeper than mere friendship, until now he had said nothing.

"I was hoping you'd suggest that very thing," he said lightheartedly.

Hanna's spirits sank as she realized he had misinterpreted her meaning and thought she was interested in him. "I believe we are only friends."

"Good friends, I might add," Ryan interjected.

"It's not a good idea to read anything else into our relationship."

"But I already have," he stated. "I'd like for us to pray about a more permanent arrangement."

Hanna took a deep breath. "No, Ryan, it wouldn't work."

"Why? Don't tell me there's someone else!" Although his question sounded polite enough, she heard the surprise in his voice.

"Actually, there is," she replied firmly, "someone very special." Her heart drummed inside her chest. *Don't ask me who,* she silently begged. *Mark and I have yet to talk!*

Ryan stopped on the trail, while Hanna ran on a few feet ahead of him, then circled back to run in place. His crystal blue eyes narrowed as they bore into hers. She despised confrontations, and here she stood in the middle of one. He lifted his chin in determination.

"We run every morning—six days a week, and not once have you ever mentioned seeing another guy," he began, his words coming out in a rush. "We've gone out a few times, and it seemed to me that you had a good time. Right now, I feel a little foolish, but not enough to give up."

"I don't know what to say," she finally admitted, still keeping pace. She knew, out of courtesy and respect, that she should stop running, but she couldn't will her legs to halt.

"Would you stop for one minute?" Ryan insisted, his voice frazzled.

Hanna instantly stood still. "I'm sorry, that was rude."

He wiped the sweat from his forehead. "Please, hear me out. I want you to have the best, and I want you to be happy, but I'm asking you to give me a chance."

"It's no use," she said gently.

"How can you be so sure?" He shook his head and wiped the sweat dripping from his forehead. "I'm asking for an opportunity to show you how much I care. Now, I know real love is a give and take for both people, but I'm willing to do all the work for now. . .so you'll see I'm serious."

She pressed her lips firmly together. "You don't want that kind of a relationship, Ryan, not really. You deserve a girl who will love you completely. I'm not the one for you. What you're asking isn't fair to either of us. And I don't believe your suggestion is what God desires for two people."

"I agree completely, and I hope I'm not coming across like a lovesick kid who can't handle a simple no. But would you not close your mind to us right this minute? I'd really like for you to give this some thought while you're on the mission trip. Then when you get back we can talk. I really care about you, Hanna, and well, we can discuss this further after your trip."

"I don't think there's anything to discuss," Hanna insisted. She shook her head and contemplated heading back to the apartment. Being with Ryan in the middle of this discussion made her feel uneasy, but the problem needed to be resolved. She knew what it was like to be rejected from her past pent-up feelings about Mark, and she didn't want to deliberately hurt Ryan. Perhaps she should start getting her morning exercise at another time. The thought of using the treadmill at the church's workout facility crept across her mind.

"I promise you this," he began. "If you tell me after the trip that your heart is definitely with this guy, I won't bother you again. In fact, I'll even start running somewhere else."

Hanna pondered his words. Whether the final decision was made now or later, she knew nothing would change. She had been in love with Mark for too long.

"And I won't bring up the subject again, unless you do. So we can continue running together the rest of the week without either of us feeling uncomfortable."

She hesitated, wanting an easy way out of the problem and yet wishing it could all be settled right now. "I don't anticipate any change. Maybe *I* should change my exercise time."

"No," he quickly said. "I started this whole thing, and I should be the one to back off and give you space. Besides, you were here each morning long before I showed up. I'll do something different the rest of this week. If it's all right with you, I'd like to call Thursday night when you get back and see if you've changed your mind."

"I can live with that," she slowly agreed.

"Good!" Ryan smiled, then took a quick glance at his watch. "I've got to go. Early morning rounds today." He paused, and his blue eyes captured her gaze, coming to rest on her lips. For a breathless second, Hanna feared he'd try to kiss her, but he didn't. "I'll be praying for you and the mission trip. Take care, and I'll talk to you soon."

Hanna waved good-bye as he headed toward his car. With a heavy sigh, she realized she had hurt him, but he had to hear the truth. A matter of days wouldn't make a bit of difference.

She remembered speaking of Mark many times to Ryan, but only in the context of their working relationship. Odd that he had no inkling of their growing friendship. Or maybe Ryan hadn't wanted to suspect anything.

Breaking into a slow jog, she attempted to rid her mind of uneasiness and move on to more pleasant thoughts. This being Wednesday, tonight the youth planned to rehearse their musical and work out some of the rough spots. The basses and altos were still having a difficult time on one song in particular, and a girl who had a critical role in the drama planned to be on vacation with her parents. Hanna remembered how well the students sounded at the church's anniversary celebration, and she had no doubts about an excellent performance at the camp in Progreso.

Navy blue T-shirts, with the newly adopted logo of Christfire, had arrived yesterday, a guarantee that all the students would be at rehearsal tonight. Several of the kids had worked together to design the symbol, a huge torch rising out of a blazing fire, with the name Christfire above it. They were so excited about the trip, especially their teaching duties in vacation Bible school.

And a whole eleven days with Mark. Hanna smiled. Maybe, just maybe, they might have a chance to talk.

He had phoned yesterday morning at the church office, and they had visited briefly. It was the first time he had had an opportunity to call since their conversation on Saturday night. He had thought he might have extra time on Sunday, but some of the pastors elected to do evangelism work in the afternoon, and he got back to the hotel in barely enough time to attend the evening worship services. Full of enthusiasm, he told her the pastors' conference propelled nonstop, with several sessions going on at the same time. Sleep proved nonexistent, but he loved every minute of it.

He had told her quickly about the Bennetts, and she nearly cried. The last few days she found herself either embarrassingly giddy or crying over the smallest things.

After work, Hanna arrived home, intending to play piano and read before meeting with the youth. She felt anxious, restless, and ecstatic, and she knew the reason centered around Mark. The way he'd kissed her. . .the tenderness she saw in his eyes when they parted on Saturday. The way he laughed. The gentle sound of his voice when he spoke her name. The newness of love cast a special glow over her world.

Sitting at the piano, she closed her eyes and played classical selections from memory. Gradually her mind and heart slowed its maddening pace, and she allowed herself to dream, just a little, about Mark.

The sound of the doorbell startled her, and for a moment she feared Ryan had decided to pay a visit. *Surely not,* she told herself. *He isn't the type of man to go back on his word.*

Curious and yet cautious, she hesitated before opening the door. *Oh, Lord, if it's him, give me the right words to say.*

"Who's there?"

"Deliveryman, miss. I have a package for Miss Hanna Stewart."

Oh, Ryan, not again, she inwardly moaned. *Where's your self-respect?* She slowly turned the knob and smiled faintly at the young man holding a long white box.

"Miss Stewart?" he asked with a wide grin.

"Yes." Realizing the poor fellow couldn't be blamed for

Ryan Henderson's persistence, she broadened her smile.

"These are for you." He carefully laid the box in her arms. "Enjoy the flowers."

She thanked him and stepped back inside her apartment. For a moment she wondered if she should have refused them. Laying the box on the kitchen table, she deliberated whether to open it or not. Staring at the box, she reluctantly lifted the cover.

"Oh," she murmured, and her hand flew to her mouth. "How beautiful."

The delicate scent of a dozen long-stemmed red roses tantalized her senses. They were by far the most lovely she'd ever seen. Hanna didn't want to touch a single petal; she felt it betrayed her love for Mark.

A small white envelope rested at the side of the box. Dare she open it? Trembling, she picked it up and held it tightly between her fingers. *I've got to call and tell him emphatically that this has got to stop. These must have cost a fortune.*

Pulling out the enclosed card, she took a deep breath and read: *I miss you more than ever. How about dinner Saturday night? Love, Mark.*

seventeen

For Saturday's dinner date Hanna chose a long, straight sundress in a black and wine print that hugged her slim figure. She clasped her hair at the crown and allowed the curls to cascade down her back. Her naturally curly hair used to drive her crazy, especially in the high humidity. But after college, she had decided to grow it out and let it have its own way. She loved the look and found the style simpler to manage.

Rummaging through her jewelry box, she selected a gold, twisted rope choker, matching bracelet and earrings, a gift from her parents when she received her master's in music. For a moment she toyed with the idea of calling and telling them about her and Mark's blossoming relationship. *No, I'll see them Sunday afternoon,* she decided, fastening the jewelry into place.

Next she slipped into black open-toe heels and stuffed a tiny black evening bag with lipstick, a tissue, and her wallet. After lightly applying her favorite perfume to her wrists and behind her ears, she stepped back to catch a glimpse of herself in the floor-length mirror. She couldn't help but notice the heightened color in her cheeks.

Mark Alexander, you bring out more color in me than an extra dab of blush, she thought happily.

Mark phoned from the apartment's security gate. This was her cue to meet him in the parking lot. Above all things, Hanna did not want Mark to be the center of ugly gossip. If anyone saw his car in the complex, he would be there with it.

She hurried to the door, then remembered her keys. Cramming them inside her too-full bag, she took a deep breath and slowly walked down the outer stairs to meet her date.

As he exited the car, she saw he wore her favorite navy blue suit, the one that cast a gold hue in the light. *You are incredibly handsome,* she thought, feeling her heart flutter. *And I'm so lucky.*

Their eyes met, and his ardent gaze sent her heart into a spin. He went around to the passenger's side and opened the door. With a wide gesture and an even broader smile, he bent low to usher her inside.

"Milady, your carriage awaits you," he whispered, taking her hand and lifting it to his lips. "You look absolutely gorgeous."

"Thank you." She tingled from his touch. "And you must be my knight in shining armor."

"None other," he murmured. "I am at your disposal for the evening."

How about a lifetime? She felt her cheeks flush and couldn't think of a single clever response.

Mark grinned, and she saw her reflection in his brown eyes. "Do you have everything you need?" he asked softly.

"Indeed I do," she replied with a giggle. "I have my knight and my carriage."

The ambiance of the evening continued as the two dined at an elegant seafood and steak restaurant in the Galleria section of Houston. They ate by amber candlelight in their own special world. She indeed felt like a princess. She wished the evening could go on forever.

After dinner they strolled hand in hand past elite shopping areas, commenting on window displays and exquisite fashions, laughing uncontrollably over everything until they reached a popular bookstore. Inside they examined everything from various titles of music to the latest fiction releases for children.

"Are you ready for coffee and conversation?" Mark asked, pulling a book from a shelf marked *Christianity*.

"Sounds wonderful," Hanna said. "But I think I'd like to pay for my novel first."

"Let me get it for you," he insisted. "Tonight's all my treat."

He looked over her shoulder to view the title. "What did you select?"

Hanna laughed and quickly covered the paperback with her hand. When he attempted to read between her fingers, she relinquished her hold with a blush. "You win. It's a Christian romance to read on the way to Progreso. A bus ride with teenagers requires a definite escape plan."

"Hmm, my thoughts exactly." His eyes sparkled.

"Why? What are you purchasing?"

"Oh, a biography on C. S. Lewis—to read on the trip to Progreso."

They both laughed as Mark set her book on top of his, and they made their way to the cashier.

"Do you mind if we drive back to our side of town to the coffee shop across from the mall?" he asked, pulling his wallet from inside his jacket.

"Not at all." She flashed her best smile.

Moments later they retrieved their car and headed toward the mall area.

"Here's hoping the entire youth group doesn't show up." He chuckled then added more seriously, "If it's all right with you, I'd like a private table outside so we can talk." He reached across the car seat and took her hand into his; his warmth spreading like liquid fire through her veins. "We've got a long overdue conversation about *us* in order."

"Sounds like an excellent idea." His tone sent her heart fluttering.

Pulling into the parking area of the coffee shop, she noticed the inside buzzed with activity, but the outside held few customers.

"Would you look at all those empty tables?" Mark asked, as though reading her mind. "What a great plan."

Once inside, he ordered a double espresso, and she ordered a vanilla nut decaf. Making their way through the busy crowd, they chose a secluded table away from the storefront with only a glimmer of light.

"Perfect spot," Mark commented, removing his jacket and placing it around his chair. "Perfect night, and a perfect lady."

She felt strangely quiet and a bit shaky. Knowing he would lead the conversation, that he was the one in charge, rattled her. Her past preference for maintaining control of every situation nibbled at her. She sipped nervously on her coffee and prayed that her jitters would calm. She felt his eyes studying her and realized he looked as frazzled as she. Smothering a giggle, she watched him prop his feet on the extra chair across from them.

He shook his head. "Hanna, I had a whole speech prepared, and now I can't remember what to say or where to begin—and that's coming from a preacher."

Hanna smiled and glanced down at her cup. "Why not at the beginning—with prayer?" she suggested shyly, lifting her chin to face him.

"Yeah, you're right." He promptly removed his feet from the chair and moved closer to her. Taking her hand in his, he momentarily stared off into the night. Clearing his throat, he bowed his head to pray. "Lord God, we come to You with open hearts to talk—to see if You desire a relationship between us other than friendship. We ask Your blessing, wisdom, and guidance in whatever You desire for us. Amen." Lifting his head, he touched her nose with his forefinger and smiled.

Releasing a long breath, he leaned back in his chair. "You know, when I think about me in high school," he began earnestly, "and how lost and aimless my life was then, I'm completely overwhelmed at what God did for me. He saved me from myself and then called me into the ministry. Now I see that every step of the way He had another purpose, not only to mold me into a more godly man, but also to prepare me for a deeper relationship with a special lady. Only God could have caused those events to take place. Only God in His divine scheme of things could have seen us in the past and planned for the future."

Hanna's heart thumped wildly, and she willed it to slow down. She knew he could feel her hands quivering in his.

"I heard a speaker say once that God is the poet, and we are the poem. As He writes the lines of our lives, and makes them rhyme, that is a miracle in itself. The way He orchestrated my leaving Dallas and coming to Abundant Grace Church still amazes me. I believe He wanted me in Houston, not only to minister to the students but also to reestablish our friendship." He chuckled. "Remember when I first saw you again after all those years? Well, I honestly didn't recognize you. I went home thinking I'd just met an angel, and I had. God led me to you; I'm sure of it."

Hanna smiled, memorizing every word and tone of his voice. *Thank You, Lord, for this. For fulfilling the desires of my heart.* Breathlessly she focused on Mark again.

"The more time I spent with you, the more I respected your walk with the Lord, your commitment to the students, and your effortless giving." He inhaled deeply. "And something else happened to me, too. I couldn't think of you any longer as an old friend. You had stolen my heart." All the while he spoke, his thumb gently stroked the back of her hand, sending shivery sensations throughout her.

Lost in the tenderness of his gaze, she bit her lower lip and blinked back the tears threatening to spill over her cheeks.

"But I couldn't tell how you felt, and that bothered me night and day. I looked forward to our evening phone conversations. . .just hearing your voice brightened every day. Some days I thought you cared, and other days. . .well, I simply couldn't tell. I tried to tell myself that if someone else was in your life, I should be happy and wish you the best. But I really wanted you all to myself."

Hanna turned her fingers, held so gently in his grasp, to

entwine with his. Staring into his beloved eyes, a single tear escaped, and he lightly brushed it away.

With a slight squeeze of her hand, he spoke again. "So then I prayed for my selfish, jealous attitude and God's will for both our lives. At camp I couldn't stand not knowing any longer, so I had to call and find out." He paused. "Then I blew it by letting the little green monster out again."

Slowly floating back to earth, Hanna shook her head. "Mark, we both know the danger of selfishness and jealousy, but I want you to know that I didn't go out with Ryan the night you called. I. . .I simply couldn't. I never dreamed you were interested in me. I never thought it possible," she said quietly.

"Never thought it possible?" he asked incredulously, feathering the backs of his fingers over her damp cheek. "You are the most beautiful, sweet, giving woman I have ever met." His lingering gaze etched her heart. "If I could, I'd kiss you right here," he whispered.

"And I'd kiss you right back," she replied in the same whisper, surprised she could utter anything at all.

"Can we make a go at a solid relationship?" he asked. "Have you prayed about us?"

"Actually," she said with a sigh, "I have, and the answer is yes. But I have a confession to make."

"Well, hello, you two," a male voice interrupted.

Hanna's heart sank as they glanced up to see Ryan Henderson standing before them, smiling and drinking coffee.

Mark reached out to grasp his hand, letting go of Hanna's in the process. "It's good to see you, Ryan."

"Yes, it's been awhile." His eyes studied her, and she felt the tension between her and Ryan thick enough to slice.

"How are you?" she managed.

"As well as can be expected," he slowly responded.

"Work keeping you busy?" Mark asked easily, taking Hanna's hand again.

"Always," he sighed. "How about you? I hear you have a mission trip in a couple of days."

Mark nodded. "Guess I'm taking your jogging partner from you."

"That you did." He smiled at her.

Her stomach knotted at Ryan's words. She *had* hurt him deeply.

"Well, you two have a good evening," he said with a nod of his head. "I'm with friends inside." He turned to Mark. "Take care, and I wish you the best in your ministry. . .and in your future." His eyes tore through her. "Bye, Hanna. I understand now."

As he walked away, she saw the puzzled look on Mark's face.

"We're not meeting in the mornings anymore," she explained. "He wanted a relationship that I couldn't give him."

Mark hesitated. "Does Ryan have anything to do with the confession you wanted to make earlier?"

"Not at all," she replied with a tilt of her head. "But now that I think about it, I'm not quite sure I can say it. It's pretty embarrassing."

"Try me," he urged softly. "I've already spilled my guts, and you know how I feel about you."

"Okay," she began with a deep breath. "You might as well know that I've thought about you and me together since I was sixteen years old. I used to plant myself around every one of your classes, just hoping for a glimpse."

With those words, he leaned over and placed a kiss on her cheek. "I'm a slow learner," he whispered near her ear. "Just don't tell me I'm too late."

She lost herself in the shining promises in his eyes.

eighteen

"How far is it to Progreso?" Mark asked an hour after the bus departed from the church. He and Hanna sat together in the midst of the students in hopes they could keep them somewhat calm.

Hanna lifted her eyes from her novel just in time to catch his dimpled grin, and she felt the all-too-familiar flutter in her stomach. "You remind me of one of the kids," she accused, returning his smile.

"Guess I am," he conceded. "I'm restless and excited." He brushed against her shoulder and whispered, "And I'm sitting next to my best girl, even though she has her nose stuck in a book."

"Where's your biography of C. S. Lewis?" she asked sweetly, closing the novel and forgetting everything she'd just read. Just the sound of his voice caused her to melt into the palm of his hand.

"Oh, in my backpack under the seat." He gave her a hopeless, pitiful look. "I'm not in the mood to read."

She laughed and pointed to the students in the back of the bus. "You could try singing with the kids."

"Believe me, you would regret it."

Hanna reached for her tote bag beneath the seat. "I have just the information to settle your restless spirit." She pulled out a file folder and leafed through it. "Ah, here's what you need." She placed it in his lap and began thumbing through the sheets of paper. "Now let me see. According to this, it's three hundred forty-five miles to Progreso, or about six hours and forty-five minutes. That doesn't include potty breaks or lunch, so I'd say we have about eight and a half hours on the road."

Mark looked genuinely surprised. "Where did you get this? I'm really impressed."

"A special program on my computer. It gives me instructions on the best way to drive to a specific location and the amount of time it takes to get there." She handed him another piece of paper. "This map shows our route, and this one is a blown-up version of the Harlingen area, which is larger and close to Progreso." She pointed to the small circle indicating their destination. "And that's our home for the next nine nights."

"You're quite the computer whiz."

"Not really. My dad gave me the program because I'm always getting lost. You see, I have no sense of direction." She searched through the folder until she found one last sheet and handed it to him. "This final map shows Progreso and the area surrounding it, complete with restaurants, lodging, and various businesses."

"Is there anything you've missed?" he asked good-naturedly, with a wink of his eye.

"Oh, probably so, but you can think I'm wonderful. That's okay." Hanna laughed.

"Trust me, I do." He wrinkled his nose at her and then dived into the information before him.

"If we aren't careful, this whole busload of kids will be on to us," she pointed out, with a quick glance around to see if any were observing them.

"They already are," he replied, not lifting his eyes from the papers, but his fingers lightly touched the back of her hand.

"No, they're not," she quietly insisted, yanking back her hand as though she'd just been burned. His touch sent her toes quivering in her tennis shoes and her heart pounding double time. She wondered if he had any idea what his nearness did to her.

He chuckled, then whispered, "Think about it. When do they see you or me when we're not together?"

"Oh. . .you were at camp without me," she pointed out.

She grimaced at the thought of the kids teasing them and talking about her and Mark as an item. Suddenly, she wondered if the parents suspected the same thing. "Should we do anything about it? I mean, are we being inappropriate?"

His eyes twinkled. "I have a solution, but there won't be time to discuss it until we get back home. In the meantime, you'll have to endure the giggles and remarks." He glanced around in feigned nervousness as though the students were watching and listening.

Hanna clamped her lips together to keep from saying more. "Well, I'm ready to sing with the kids," she said, thinking he would stop the ribbing if she changed the topic of conversation.

"What? No more romance novel?"

Giving him a wry smile, she willed her stomach to stop turning cartwheels. "I think it's getting me into trouble," she confessed.

And just what is your solution to all of this? she wondered. Dare she dream a little more?

Within moments after he'd warned her about the kids putting the two of them together, Preston asked Mark if he could pry himself away from Hanna long enough to answer a few questions about the trip. The student's question brought a fresh rise of color to her cheeks, but apparently Mark found it amusing.

When they finally reached the campsite at Progreso, she and Mark made certain each student matched up with a counselor and a cabin. The kids took their luggage and scattered off to make their beds and unpack their things before dinner.

His words about a possible solution to their circumstances still clung to her mind as she made up her bunk. She would be sharing a cabin with a nurse, a mother of one of the students. No doubt both women would be busy in the days to come. Mission trips, in the past, called for healing of the spirit and the body, especially with teenage boys who believed they were invincible.

The dinner bell rang and Hanna hurried to the huge building known as the mess hall. As she contemplated the sure-to-come food fights, she surmised that the building had been suitably named.

As the students and adults alike crowded around the door, Mark quieted them all for prayer. "Heavenly Father," he began, "thank You for bringing us all here safely. We ask Your blessing upon each and every one of us as we prepare our hearts to do Your work. Pour out Your Holy Spirit to bring the children to vacation Bible school. Give us the strength and wisdom to do our best. Bless this food and the hands that have prepared it. May it nourish our bodies that we may nourish your kingdom. In Jesus' holy and precious name. Amen."

The crowd formed two lines inside for spaghetti, green beans, salad, garlic bread, and chocolate cake. Hanna braced herself for ten days of starch. She had brought fresh fruit, single-cup decaf coffee, cans of tuna, and low fat soup. From past experiences, she knew the camps served nutritious meals, but their budget forced them to use less expensive menus that contained lots of fattening carbohydrates.

"Is everyone ready for a great week?" Mark called out above the roar of students laughing and talking as they finished their meal.

A roar of enthusiasm met his ears.

He stood, and his presence demanded their attention as the room slowly quieted. "Great! Let me give you the game plan for tomorrow's Sunday worship. Breakfast will be at seven with Hanna leading a praise and worship time. At nine-thirty the buses will transport each cabin, with their counselors, to different worship services in the surrounding community. The ministers of these churches will introduce you as part of a large nondenominational vacation Bible school here at the camp. At the close of the service, you will pass out fliers about our VBS, which begins Monday morning at nine and will continue through Saturday. We will accept children from ages four through fourteen with a special teen leadership class for those over age twelve.

"Your counselor will explain the rules, duties, and responsibilities tonight at devotions before going to bed. This is the only evening that we will not have a worship service. Today has been long and we're all tired, to say nothing of what is ahead of us. Each one of you will have a specific job for the week, and it's crucial that none of you decide to do any crusading on your own. In other words, stick with your cabin and obey your counselor. We have a God-sized project here, and we are thankful God has included us in His work.

"Also, we need a name for each of the twelve cabins. Try to select one tonight. During the time we spend here, we plan some sport competition between the groups. In the event of two cabins selecting the same name, well. . .first come first served." Mark took a deep breath. "Any questions?"

"What if we don't like our assigned job?" one girl asked.

"Talk to your counselor. If there's still a problem, then you and your counselor need to talk to me. By the way, Mrs. Roberts, our nurse, Hanna, and I have the only available phones. Contact us for emergency calls only. Any other questions?"

"What time does VBS end?" a boy inquired.

"One o'clock, which includes lunch at twelve-thirty for everyone. Free time is from one until supper, and supper is served at five-thirty. We will invite the children and their parents back for the evening worship service at seven-thirty."

With no more questions, Mark dismissed the group. Hanna admired his leadership abilities. In the short amount of time he had been youth minister at Abundant Grace, he had proved himself a capable and responsible leader. His love for the students and his untiring efforts to lead them spiritually drew a large crowd. She felt proud of him. Even more, she felt privileged to be working with him.

Late that night Hanna checked each of the girls' cabins while Mark did the same for the boys. Sometimes counselors had problems gaining the students' attention and respect. Tonight proved no exception.

Shortly after eleven, Hanna wearily trudged toward her cabin to find Mark waiting on the front steps. He looked excited and ready for the new day, not at all like she felt. One of the junior high girls had been quite argumentative about the "no radios" rule, and Hanna had feared she would have to call the parents. Fortunately, the girl realized Hanna was serious and begrudgingly relinquished her boom box.

Propping the radio on the ground beside her, she caught a lingering smile from Mark. Its glow scattered all the unpleasantness of dealing with an unhappy young lady.

"Have a seat," he urged, scooting to make room for her on the step.

"Don't mind if I do," she replied. "How are the guys?"

"Typical, but settled down. How about you?"

"The same," she smiled. "You know, sometimes girls are harder to deal with than boys."

He shrugged. "Want to tell horror stories and find out?"

"That's okay," she conceded with a smile. "I just came from one, but it turned out all right."

"Should I tell you about my worst camp experience?" Mark asked with a laugh.

She instantly fell under his spell. He had a soothing air about him that lifted her spirits. "By all means. I want to hear all about it."

"Well, it was a senior citizens' group."

She looked askance at him. "You're kidding? How could those sweet elderly people be a problem? What happened?"

Mark shook his head and chuckled. "For starters, the men stole shortening from the kitchen and spread it all over the ladies' clean white sheets."

"Senior citizens? How awful."

"Oh, yes," he replied. "The ladies retaliated by filling the men's shoes with mud. Then the men swiped all the toilet tissue from the ladies' restroom. The entire week sported one prank after another."

"What did you do?" Hanna asked, laughing so hard her sides ached, trying to subdue herself before she woke the entire camp.

"Nothing, absolutely nothing. I couldn't threaten to send them home. Who to? They even told grandchildren jokes," Mark groaned. "And I got the brunt of all their teasing."

"I'd expect older folks to be settled and full of wisdom, ready to be mentors for younger Christians," she giggled.

Mark's eyes grew wide. "Oh, they were, absolutely sweet and helpful—until one of them got a crazy idea."

Once the merriment ceased, the two discussed camp business. Three cabins had chosen the same name, a popular Christian singing group.

"I think, since they all chose a music group, you should handle it," Mark claimed.

"And since you are the youth minister, you should do the honors," Hanna hastily replied.

Mark sighed with a dramatic shrug. "Okay, we'll both take care of it in the morning. Hey, you know what?" he asked, picking up her hand and weaving his fingers through hers. "Wouldn't it be great to have Josie here?"

Hanna nodded sadly. "Yeah, it would. One of the high school girls said the same thing earlier. Wish we knew more about her. Poor thing, she always seemed cold."

"What do you mean?"

Hanna tilted her head reflectively. "Didn't you ever notice how she always wore long sleeves and jeans year-round? Made me think she was lacking something both spiritually and physically."

Mark looked at her oddly.

"What are you thinking?" she asked.

He gave her hand a gentle squeeze. "I'm not sure," he said hesitantly, "and I'd rather not say until I think this through." He drew her hand to his lips and kissed it lightly. "Let's call it a night, sweet lady. You and I need all the rest we can get."

"You're right. I could sit here all night talking to you, but my eyes feel like they're held open with toothpicks."

He squeezed her hand again and pulled her to her feet. "Due to our present environment, any future hugs and kisses will have to be postponed until we get back home."

She smiled, suppressing her regret. "I'll send you some through osmosis."

"Wonderful." He touched her cheek with his knuckle. "See you bright and early."

Cherishing the memory of that brief touch, Hanna literally fell into bed. She marveled at the number of students who had found the money to fund the trip. They were all enthusiastic and ready to take on the next nine days. She wanted to concentrate on the week's activities and focus on praying for the students, but she couldn't stay awake. So much to do in such a short time. . . .

nineteen

Sunday's events flowed smoothly, and several of the churches provided transportation for the children during the six days of vacation Bible school. The week would end with an outdoor service on Sunday, followed by a picnic and games for everyone. Mark made certain all of the literature had been printed in Spanish and English so the parents could read what their children were learning.

Preston proved a valuable help as he assisted one of the adults with a cabin full of junior high boys rather than bunking with guys his own age. Hanna watched him grow closer to Mark. At first she felt a pang of jealousy, for her former student had always come to her with his questions and concerns. But as he turned to Mark for advice and leadership, she realized Preston needed the companionship of a godly man.

"Aren't these kids great?" Mark asked on Tuesday evening after cabin check. He and Hanna had been discussing the more than one hundred children involved in Bible school.

Hanna smiled in agreement. "They're like little sponges soaking up all the love and laughter we can give them. Even though most of the younger ones only speak Spanish, they all know the name of Jesus."

"Yesterday nearly a dozen children made decisions for Jesus, and last night three families came forward," Mark pointed out. "By any chance, would you have time in the morning to help me follow up with the new believers? I'd like to get the children and adults connected to one of the local churches."

"Sure. Now that the students know the routine, I'm free to roam around and collect hugs from the little ones." Watching his face, she had to smile. She loved the energy and enthusiasm in this man, and she knew it came from the Lord.

"This is all so good for our kids. All the books and teachers in the world cannot take the place of experiencing God's love firsthand."

Hanna nodded. "I've never been so happy and at peace. It's tempting to stay here forever."

"I know how you feel—kind of like a glimpse of heaven." He added softly, "It's like being with you."

Hanna wished she could see his eyes, but they were hidden by the shadows of night. "Thank you for the compliment."

He clasped her hand with both of his. "You're welcome, but it's the truth." When he spoke again, his voice was husky. "Hanna, have you ever considered what it would be like. . . married to a minister?"

She felt her heart skip a beat. Of course, she had thought about it! Every idle moment, she thought about Mark and a possible future with him. She took a deep breath and prayed for her words to be steady. "Well," she began slowly, "I've wondered about it. I can see a minister's time is not his own. Probably similar to a doctor."

"But unlike a doctor's income, a pastor's income is limited," he said soberly, turning her hand over in his, nervously. "Sacrifices of time and money are all too common. In many instances, the wife is expected to take a support role both at home and at church. Her responsibilities can be as overwhelming as his, especially when children are involved."

Hanna swallowed hard. She didn't know whether to speak in specifics or in generalities. She chose the latter. "I believe there are problems and difficult circumstances in any marriage, whether the couple is in ministry or working in the secular world. The couple must realize that God is the head of the family and trust His guidance in whatever work He has called them to do."

"I agree," Mark said with a sigh. "I've seen some ministers' marriages fail because their wives didn't understand their husbands' position—or when he simply forgot his commitment to her. . .and she came last, which is not God's will. . . I was just wondering about your thoughts on the matter."

"Are you doing a special study?" she asked quietly, yet teasingly. Normally she wouldn't react so boldly, but their relationship had soared during the past few days.

He grinned, easing the tension between them. "Yeah, you might call it that."

"Keep me posted on your findings."

"Believe me, you will be the first to know," he answered more seriously, without a trace of humor. He lifted her hand to his lips and kissed it lightly. "Thank you, for blessing my life."

She blinked back the tears flooding her eyes. So much she wanted to say. . .so much she wanted him to say. Questions poured from her heart. What did he want from their relationship? Sometimes she just felt like grabbing his hand and running to a remote site deep in a thick forest where no one could bother them. Maybe then they could talk about everything. Maybe, for once, she could be completely honest about her deep, growing love for him.

As Mark had predicted, the students whispered, giggled, and teased them about a suspected romance. The couple merely ignored the comments and shook their heads, as though the thought were ludicrous.

The week progressed as the children and students worked on crafts, stories, games, and songs about Jesus. The students eagerly related their experiences, and Mark and Hanna deemed each story as important as the next. During the evening services more and more families attended the worship hour, and the number of decisions for Christ moved the whole camp to rejoice.

"One of the ministers in the area invited us back next summer," Mark told Hanna on Saturday morning at breakfast. "God is really doing a mighty work here."

"I've seen more and more mothers cry at their child's eagerness to embrace the Lord," Hanna replied, sipping black coffee. "And yesterday, a father with tears in his eyes thanked me in Spanish for his little boy's conversion."

By Saturday night, all of them began to feel the effects of little sleep and long days. Yet once again decisions were made for Christ. Sunday morning worship services were packed inside and outside the open chapel area. Several churches had decided to hold their services at the campsite and join the festivities afterward. Despite scraped elbows, bee stings, poison ivy, and the usual round of stomach disorders, the week had been a success

During the noon picnic of hotdogs, buttery corn on the cob, chips, watermelon, ice cream, and brownies, Preston asked to talk with Mark and Hanna privately.

"What's up, guy?" Mark asked, as they sat beneath a tree away from the crowd.

Preston seemed to search for the right words, and the two waited patiently for him to speak.

"First off," he began, "outside my family, you two are my most favorite people." His blue eyes turned toward her. "Hanna, you loved me when I didn't love myself. You showed me Jesus in your actions, and I'll always be grateful for what you did for my family. Without your persistence, none of us would know the Lord. You encouraged me with my music and always gave more than I could give back." He focused on Mark next while Hanna fought her emotions. "You have shown me what a godly man is all about. I've listened to your testimony and your messages, and I thank God for putting you into my life. This whole week I've been struggling with something—something God has been trying to tell me, so I want to tell you both about it." He took a deep breath. "God has called me into the music ministry, and tonight I accepted His plan for my life."

"Oh, Preston, what wonderful news," Hanna cried, reaching to embrace the young man. "Your mother will be so proud.

Goodness, *I'm* so proud."

Mark took his turn at hugging him and congratulating him on his obedient step of faith. All three of them held hands and prayed for the young man's direction.

"Now," Preston said with a twinkle of mischief in his eyes, "when you two decide to get married, I want to be the first to know."

Mark eyed him suspiciously and chuckled. "I think an answer to that would have this whole camp talking."

Hanna reached up and ruffled Preston's blond hair. "I agree with the pastor here. But if anything changes, we'll let you know." Mark caught her eye with a wink.

❧

The road sign said fifty miles to Houston. Hanna glanced over at Mark sleeping beside her. He looked so relaxed, and she envied his serene state. Her mind spun wildly with all the week's events. The past ten days of joys and accomplishments kept her head swarming with bits and pieces of conversations—and always laughing, affectionate children. Now all of them must encounter reality again, but their memories would live on. The students had grown tremendously, and she sensed a new height of maturity in many of them. They had given themselves to serve a community that needed fresh, unconditional love. Hanna praised God for allowing her to see another one of His miracles.

At the church, parents greeted the exhausted but excited students as they filed off the buses. Pastor Jacobs welcomed the group back and helped the kids secure their luggage. One by one they picked up their belongings and headed home full of stories and reports of new friends. The pastor, Mark, and Hanna waved good-bye until the parking lot stood empty.

"I have someone in my office waiting to see you two," the pastor said with a smile.

"Who could that be?" Mark asked curiously.

"David and Linda Bennett."

Mark and Hanna exchanged quick glances. She wanted to believe it meant a turn for the best.

"Is Josie with them?" she asked.

"No, but I'll let them explain everything."

As they entered Pastor Jacobs' office, Hanna and Mark greeted the Bennetts. Hanna thought the couple looked rested, peaceful, and calm. She herself felt nervous and incredibly anxious.

"I'm glad you two came," David began. "I certainly wouldn't have blamed you if you passed on this one."

"I believe I speak for both of us. We may be confused, but we're not angry," Mark replied.

"Well, I'm not so certain I could be understanding in your shoes. Linda and I apologize for the abrupt manner in which we handled our daughter's illness. Decisions had to be made quickly, and we went solely on the advice of Josie's psychiatrist, not that we agreed with everything he said, but we were desperate to have her condition treated."

"Can you tell us about Josie?" Hanna asked. "Is she all right?"

David grasped his wife's hand and smiled before speaking. "To tell you about her, we must go back to the night she overdosed. There was more to the story than the suicide attempt."

"I have to take the blame for some of it," Linda interrupted and looked up into her husband's face. "Can I begin?" When he nodded, she took a deep breath. "We knew something was terribly wrong with Josie, and at first we feared drugs. But we noticed that each time she ate or we confronted her about a particular behavior, she disappeared into the bathroom. I thought food disorder or drug abuse, and that night I walked into the bathroom to find out for sure. What I found sickened me." She started to cry, and her husband embraced her shoulders.

"Josie is a cutter," David said quietly. "Are you familiar with this disorder?"

Mark nodded, but Hanna shook her head. "I've never heard

of it," she replied.

"In short, it's a form of self-mutilation in which the person cuts herself with whatever sharp instrument she can find. The injuries are usually made between the wrist and the forearm and sometimes on the legs. It's not an attempt to commit suicide but a type of self-punishment when the person is upset or feels out of control."

Hanna's hand flew to her mouth. "That's why she always wore long sleeves and jeans!"

"Right," he replied. "And we had no idea she had fallen victim to this until her mother walked in on her."

"I didn't handle it well at all," Linda admitted. "My initial reaction to seeing her slash her arm was anger. I knew nothing about the disorder and thought she'd discovered another way to get attention. I screamed and shouted, said horrible things. I even told her that if she really contemplated suicide then her attempts were useless." She took a deep breath and Hanna handed her a tissue. "Well, she proved me wrong, as we well know. David heard every word, but he didn't know how to respond. We argued up until the time you called and alerted us to her overdose."

"I'm not sure if the doctor gave us sound counsel by isolating her from those who cared about her. We both felt Ryan Henderson had made excellent progress, but again we were desperate enough to follow anyone who promised hope. Even when it involved turning our backs on the church."

Hearing her husband's confession, Linda sobbed harder, and Hanna swallowed a lump in her throat.

"Where is your daughter now?" Mark asked.

"In a hospital in Chicago," David replied. "She's undergoing treatment with other kids, mostly young girls, who have the same disorder. In educating ourselves about Josie's illness, we've found that her self-injury is due to severe emotional pain—a means of control when the world around her becomes unbearable."

"I feel so sorry for her, for you," Hanna managed, remembering the pain of being overweight and the brunt of vicious teasing. Her sudden emotional outbursts had caused her parents to quarrel, almost separate at one time.

"It's been a long uphill climb, but with God's help, the three of us will beat this thing and be a family again," David said confidently.

"We will be in prayer," Mark assured him. "And am I safe to presume this information is just between us?"

"Yes," Linda breathed, "if you don't mind. When the time comes, Josie wants to tell the other kids about it, a testimony to God's saving grace. And, yes," the woman smiled, "Josie has surrendered her life to Jesus Christ."

"Wonderful," Hanna murmured. "And what great news for you."

"Praise God," Mark replied. "Well, I understand how you would want us to keep this information to ourselves. Is there anything we can do?"

David smiled. "Continue to keep us in your prayers."

"Then let's pray right now," Mark suggested, and they bowed their heads on Josie's behalf, thanking God for the young girl's decision for Christ and asking Him for complete healing for the Bennett family.

Afterward, as Hanna and Mark reflected upon Josie's illness, she remembered his reaction to the girl wearing clothing to cover her arms and legs.

"You already had an idea about her problem, didn't you?" she asked.

"I suspected as much, but I didn't want to make a hasty call," he said. "Sad, isn't it? If things like this happen in Christian families, imagine the heartache in families who don't know Jesus."

"Guess we have a lot of work to do," she said softly, feeling his eyes upon her.

"Yes, we do." And she saw tears in his eyes.

twenty

The next morning Hanna arrived at the church office just before noon. Mark had called earlier asking if they could have lunch together and talk, and she assumed the matter had something to do with the mission trip. Greeting the receptionist at the front office, she gathered up the mail that had accumulated in her absence and lingered a few moments answering questions about the past week. Piling the mail into her arms, she headed back to Mark's office.

"Hi, Hanna," Nancy greeted with her usual cheery smile. "Did you get caught up on your sleep last night?"

Hanna nodded then grinned. "I think so, but I really had a rough time getting out of bed this morning."

"Well, Mark is exhausted. He said the mission trip was 'awesome,' and he talked about it most of the morning. And you," she said with a sideways glance, "glow from the inside out. No need asking if you enjoyed Progreso; it's beaming from your face."

They both laughed.

"We all had a great time. I'm really thankful so many of the students were able to see God among those people. What they experienced will last a lifetime." She glanced toward Mark's closed door. "Is he busy?"

"He's on the phone."

"I'll just wait here and go through my mail," Hanna replied, easing into a wingback chair near Nancy's desk. "Do you mind?"

"No, of course not. Oh, did I tell you I met your father?"

Hanna looked up in surprise. "No, when did this happen?"

The secretary thought for a moment. "I guess he stopped

in right before youth camp. Oh, yes, now I remember. He came on your day off."

Hanna wondered why her dad hadn't mentioned the visit. He usually told her everything.

"He seems like a wonderful man," the secretary went on. "And obviously very generous."

"What do you mean?" Hanna asked, her interest aroused.

Nancy shrugged her shoulders. "Mark said he had given him a rather large check." Her eyes grew wide. "Oops, I wasn't supposed to say a word about that. I hope I haven't made a serious mistake."

"I'm sure you haven't," Hanna replied weakly, feeling her whole body tremble and her stomach begin to churn. Her mind spun with old memories of yet another check to Mark. *Why would Dad give him money?* She looked up hesitantly. "Did he say anything else about it?"

"Uh, no, not really. Oh, goodness, I feel terrible about this. I shouldn't have said a word."

"Don't you worry about a thing. I'm sure there's a good reason why they didn't want me to know," Hanna mumbled. She stood up from the chair, feeling numb. She needed time alone to sort through the doubts and misgivings that threatened to destroy her trust in Mark and her father. "I can wait to see Mark." Her voice wavered. "I just remembered something I need to do."

She dropped the mail, stooped to pick it up, and hurried to the refuge of her own office without bidding Nancy good-bye. With a ragged breath, she unlocked the door and closed it behind her. The whole affair of the last cotillion flashed vividly across her mind. She ached all over, from a pounding throb in her temples to an increasing discomfort in the pit of her stomach.

A flood of tears washed over her, despite her efforts to stop them. The old painful glimpses of the past cut into her heart as vivid as yesterday. . . She was a child again, a young girl, then a teenager, trying desperately to ignore the jeers and taunts about her weight. Hurling accusations echoed around her, the old thoughts, and the old fears. She felt herself slipping into a wretched pool of misery as the voices from the past blared through her memory.

Hey, Hippo Hanna. . . Hungry, hungry Hanna, eats a ton of bananas. . . You're unlovable. . .disgusting. . .couldn't pay someone to be your friend. . . Hanna's gaze swept around the room, so absorbed in the despair that she failed to call out for the One who had always loved her.

"Jesus," she whispered at last through her tears. "Forgive me for not clinging to You. I know in Your eyes I'm worthy, completely loved, and a delight to my heavenly Father. Jesus, Jesus, help me. I'm so confused."

She fell to the floor as the sobs shook her frame. With all of her might, she prayed for peace and a focus on others instead of herself. She reflected upon Josie and the teen's struggle to fight an addictive behavior. The faces of joyous children and adults in Progreso who had surrendered their lives to Christ were a reason to rejoice. Some of the students from Abundant Grace had never seen poverty before, but they had given themselves to answer the call of Christ.

Suddenly, a warm, peaceful sensation rested on her shoulders. Her body relaxed, and a source of strength beyond human comprehension spread a tender message of love. The fog of doubt cleared from her head. Reaching for a tissue on her desk, she dabbed her eyes and breathed a prayer of thankfulness for the victory God had just brought her through.

I am beyond this sort of thing, she firmly repeatedly to herself. *And so is Mark. None of us were Christians then, not me, Dad, or Mark.* Sitting at her desk, she began to fervently pray. *Oh, Lord God in heaven. I know there's an explanation for this, but I'm bewildered by it all. Help me to think clearly and find the answers without accusing Mark or Dad of anything unscrupulous.*

Phoning her father was a temptation, except what would

she say? The former Hanna might have driven to her parents' home in a fit of rage, or even created an ugly scene at the church office. But Christ had made her a new creation, and she refused to succumb to old ways.

Instead, Hanna opened her Bible. It occurred to her that if Mark's secretary hadn't mentioned her father's visit, she would have never known about the check. But maybe she *was* supposed to discover it, to work through the prior things that once held her in bondage and still continued to haunt her. She needed to put the past aside forever.

Her eyes embraced the words *Holy Bible*. . . God speaking to believers through the penmanship of His servants. She knew the passage she wanted to read, the same one that sustained her in the beginning when Christ first drew her to Himself. Opening the Bible to the New Testament, she found 2 Corinthians 5:16–17. "So from now on we regard no one from a worldly point of view. Though we once regarded Christ in this way, we do so no longer. Therefore, if anyone is in Christ, he is a new creation; the old has gone, the new has come!" Her eyes moved on to chapter 6, verses 1 and 2. "As God's fellow workers, we urge you not to receive God's grace in vain. For he says, 'In the time of my favor I heard you, and in the day of salvation I helped you.' I tell you, now is the time of God's favor, now is the day of salvation."

Bowing her head and closing her eyes, Hanna once more sought the Father. *O God of all Creation, who sent His only Son to die for me on the cross, thank You for saving me from my sins. Forgive my foolish questions. Help my mind not to dwell on sordid memories from before I knew You. You are my strength and my redeemer. I love You, Lord. In Your precious Son's name, Jesus. Amen.*

Glancing at her purse and keys, she realized how much she wanted to flee to the isolated security of her apartment and avoid seeing a single person, especially Mark. She hated confrontations, avoided them at every turn, but sometimes they were necessary. Running solved nothing, only prolonged the inevitable. But she was not alone, her Faithful Companion held her in His loving arms, and He would sustain her.

She should march right back to Mark's office and lovingly ask him to explain her dad's check. Shaking her head, dispelling the nagging thoughts, she mustered the courage to stand. *I can do this, and I will,* she told herself victoriously.

A light rap at the door startled her, and she knew without asking that Mark stood on the other side. Her fingers dug into the desktop, and she chewed on her lower lip. He would see she had been crying.

"Yes," she replied, sounding stronger than she truly felt.

"It's Mark. Do you have a minute?"

The questioning ring of his words told her he suspected something amiss. Taking a deep breath, she seated herself. "Come in, please."

His deep brown eyes immediately captured hers. He said nothing, but she saw the worried frown that creased his forehead.

"Would you like to sit down?" she asked quietly, staring into his beloved eyes and blinking back the tears filling her own. She didn't see a hint of betrayal, but she must learn the truth.

He shut the door behind him and seated himself. "Nancy told me everything," he began slowly and deliberately. "And I need to explain your father's visit and his check."

"I'm listening," Hanna said, folding her hands in her lap. She took a deep breath and whisked away any traces of dampness beneath her eyes. Oh, how she wanted to run from him and not face any unpleasantness, but she would stay and hear the truth.

He paused. "Your dad did give me a check the week before youth camp. We had lunch together right after the anniversary celebration." Hanna nodded, remembering her father suggesting the two men get together. "Hal wanted to make an anonymous contribution to youth camp and the mission trip's scholarship fund. I wanted to tell you, but he felt you might not understand his wanting to write me a check, although it was made out to the church for the benefit of the students. Then last week when you mentioned the number of students who were able to attend the mission trip, I realized that one of us needed to tell you."

"I wish I would have known," she said with a sigh, not able to tear her gaze from his face. "I could have thanked him for his generosity, and we could have avoided this."

Mark nodded. "I'm sorry. I'm sure your thoughts immediately flew back to the incident in high school."

She gave him a sad smile. "I was trying very hard not to dwell on our 'old' selves, praying for strength and understanding. You know, Daddy has had a hard time forgiving himself about that," she replied.

He nodded. "I could tell he felt uncomfortable with any reminder of it."

She took a deep breath. "I understand his reluctance, but I'm not that selfish, inconsiderate person anymore," she insisted. "None of us are the same people we used to be."

"I agree, and both of us should have told you about his generous gift. I am so sorry for upsetting you. Oddly enough, this check business is what I wanted to discuss with you over lunch." He leaned across her desk. "I talked to your dad this morning, and we agreed you should be told. He knew you were thrilled with the number of students who participated in the summer's activities, and we both feel deceitful in not telling you the truth."

Hanna said nothing as she digested his words. She believed Mark, and given the circumstances, she understood her father's reasoning. Any type of money transfer to Mark would make him uneasy. But she knew her father had a deep compassion for teens and often contributed to various charities on their behalf.

"Hanna?" Mark asked tenderly.

"Yes," she replied, breaking her thoughts.

"Neither one of us would ever intentionally hurt you. . . We love you too much for that."

Hanna's gaze flew to his face. "What. . .what did you say?"

"I said your dad and I love you." His voice softened. "I love you."

She couldn't think of a single word to say. Mark's words stunned and warmed her at the same time.

"Would you say something?" He stood and walked around to her side of the desk. He looked grim, and it saddened her. Did he fear her rejection of his love?

She rose to meet him. "I want to hear it again," she whispered, her heart beating wildly.

"I love you, Hanna Stewart," he said firmly and wrapped his arms around her.

She heard his heart beat furiously, matching hers. "And I love you," she whispered, gazing deep into his deep brown eyes and seeing her reflection. "I've always loved you."

He put her at arm's length and his hands gently entwined with hers. "This isn't how I planned to tell you. I wanted a quiet, intimate dinner, flowers, and. . ."

"This is perfect," she insisted with a gentle sigh while a warm smile played upon her lips.

With her hands tucked securely into his, Mark bent on one knee and peered up at her. She clung to the moment. "Hanna Stewart," he said softly, "I love you with all my heart. God has placed you in my life, and I don't want to ever let you go. Will you spend the rest of your life with me? Will you marry me?"

Pure joy exploded in her heart. "Yes," she breathed. "Yes, yes, yes!"

As he rose and drew her into his embrace, she looked into his brown eyes. The old hurts from the past faded and disappeared at last in the promise of forever love.

epilogue

"Are you ready for this?" Hal Stewart whispered to Hanna.

She linked her arm into his and took a final look at the train of her white satin wedding gown. Everything looked perfect; she felt perfect. "Yes, I am," she replied confidently.

"I've looked forward to this day since you were a little girl—but not without a few regrets," he said honestly. "I'm not so sure I want to give my precious daughter away."

"But Mark is so good," she soothed, staring up at her father with pure joy radiating from her face.

"I know, I know. Truth is, I couldn't ask for a better son-in-law."

She smiled and watched as the first bridesmaid entered the sanctuary on cue to the organ's music.

"By the way," he whispered, "you are the most beautiful bride this church has ever seen."

She giggled. "I think you're prejudiced."

"Of course I am."

And the second bridesmaid stepped in time to the music.

"Are you going to be able to sing?"

Hanna wet her lips. "If I don't cry like a baby and spoil it."

"It will be lovely."

The maid of honor stepped forward, and Hanna felt her stomach flutter in anticipation.

"I love you," her father whispered. "And so does Mark. May God bless your life together."

And father and daughter walked arm in arm to meet the expectant groom.

A Letter To Our Readers

ear Reader:

In order that we might better contribute to your reading njoyment, we would appreciate your taking a few minutes to spond to the following questions. We welcome your comments nd read each form and letter we receive. When completed, please turn to the following:

Rebecca Germany, Fiction Editor
Heartsong Presents
PO Box 719
Uhrichsville, Ohio 44683

Did you enjoy reading *The Last Cotillion?*
☐ Very much. I would like to see more books
by this author!
☐ Moderately
I would have enjoyed it more if _____

_____

_____

Are you a member of **Heartsong Presents**? Yes ☐ No ☐
If no, where did you purchase this book?_____

_____

How would you rate, on a scale from 1 (poor) to 5 (superior), the cover design?_____

On a scale from 1 (poor) to 10 (superior), please rate the following elements.

_____ Heroine   _____ Plot

_____ Hero   _____ Inspirational theme

_____ Setting   _____ Secondary characters

5. These characters were special because_____

_____

_____

6. How has this book inspired your life?_____

_____

_____

7. What settings would you like to see covered in future
   Heartsong Presents books?_____

_____

_____

8. What are some inspirational themes you would like to see
   treated in future books?_____

_____

_____

9. Would you be interested in reading other **Heartsong
   Presents** titles?   Yes ☐   No ☐

10. Please check your age range:
    ☐ Under 18   ☐ 18-24   ☐ 25-34
    ☐ 35-45   ☐ 46-55   ☐ Over 55

11. How many hours per week do you read?_____

Name _____

Occupation _____

Address _____

City _____ State _____ Zip _____

Experience a family

saga that begins in 1860 when the painting of a homestead is first given to a young bride who leaves her beloved home of Laurelwood. Then follow the painting through a legacy of love that touches down in the years 1890, 1969, and finally today. Authors Sally Laity, Andrea Boeshaar, Yvonne Lehman, and DiAnn Mills have worked together to create a timeless treasure of four novellas in one collection.

paperback, 352 pages, 5 ⁷⁄₁₆" x 8"